WITCH'S
SISTER

OTHER YEARLING BOOKS YOU WILL ENJOY:

WITCH'S SISTER

Phyllis Reynolds Naylor

ILLUSTRATED BY
Gail Owens

A YEARLING BOOK

for Jennifer

WITCH'S
SISTER

chapter one

She first suspected Judith was a witch that spring when she found her looking for tadpoles in Cowden's Creek. It was how Judith was catching them that made Lynn think it. Instead of using a net, Judith simply cupped her hands in the water and crooned to them, and they swam right into her fingers. That was only the beginning, though. There were other things, too.

But it wasn't till her mother went to work the following summer, leaving Judith in charge, that Lynn's suspicions grew too big to hold in. What had possessed Mother to go to work in a hen house when she could have worked at home? It all seemed part of the same plot, somehow. She simply said one night that the time had come, and when Lynn got up in the morning, there was her mother packing paper and envelopes and stamps into a large shopping bag on the kitchen table.

Lynn sat down on a stool and surveyed the confusion. Beside the shopping bag lay two of her mother's books —*Shy River* and *A Horse Named Harry*. On the cover of each, in neat black letters, were the words, *By Sylvia Jackson Morley*. Mrs. Morley picked these up last and placed them in the sack on top of her dictionary. There were five other books already packed.

"What's happening?" Lynn asked, her voice still foggy with sleep. She was afraid her mother might be running away. There were times when Mrs. Morley was somewhat unpredictable, but at least there had always been breakfast on the table. This morning there wasn't a trace of egg or cereal anywhere.

"I'm off to my studio," Mother said, her face beaming. "Five days a week from nine to four, but I'll be home for lunch."

Lynn stared. "Mo—ther! You're not really going to work in that chicken coop!"

"It's not a coop, my dear. It's a lovely little hen house, and it even has a stove for the winter. There hasn't been a chicken in it for two years, and Mrs. Tuggle and I have cleaned it thoroughly. When I've got it all arranged, you'll have to come see it."

"But you've always worked at home before!" Lynn protested. "You have that little corner in the sewing room, and you can go up there and shut the door and . . ."

". . . and five minutes later Stevie opens it because he wants a cookie, or you open it to ask if you can go to Marjorie's, or Judith opens it to get the pinking shears or the thread. For thirteen years I've been writing in bits and pieces—a few hours here, a few hours there—and nobody considers it working. Now that you girls are old enough to take over here at home, I've decided to rent a place where I can write undisturbed. Besides"— she stopped packing and tested the sack to make sure she could carry it—"I'm getting away from my own interruptions as well. Sometimes, when a book's going poorly, I come downstairs and clean the oven or sort through the unmatched socks. Now I won't have any excuses to get away, will I?" She smiled and leaned over to give Lynn a quick hug.

Something ghostlike in a white gown appeared in the doorway and was gone again. Lynn jerked her head just in time to see Judith going past. That was another thing. Judith never seemed to make a sound when she went somewhere. She just came on, like an apparition. Bodily transportation. Wasn't that what the witches called it?

Mrs. Morley looked at her watch. "Well, I'd better be off. I've got just seven minutes to get there with this shopping bag, and it's uphill all the way."

"Who's going to care if you're three minutes late?"

"I care," Mother said firmly. "There will be no last minute delays to fix somebody a slice of toast. Once I give in to that, I'll never get out the door."

"But what about us?" Lynn bleated, her stomach rumbling under her striped pajamas.

"Breakfast is on the back porch this morning. I thought you might enjoy it there. I'll be home about twelve to get lunch. And listen, darling—during the six hours I'm gone each day, you girls are equally responsible for Stevie. If there's any disagreement, however, it's Judith who has the final say."

"Ju—dith!" Lynn wailed.

"Yes, because she's oldest. You'll both find a list of jobs and responsibilities on the closet door, and I expect you to read them every morning before you go any-where." She stopped and looked over with an amused smile that Lynn could not share. "Why so glum? Look at it as an adventure! Who knows what the rest of the summer will bring?" Then, picking up her bulging sack, Mrs. Morley walked to the front door, kicked open the screen with one foot, staggered across the porch, down the steps, across the lawn, down more steps to the sidewalk below, and then, weaving slightly, started up the steep hill to Mrs. Tuggle's.

Stevie was still asleep, and the house seemed unusu-ally quiet for nine o'clock on a July morning. Nine more weeks of summer. Nine weeks of six hours a day with Judith? Nine weeks of Judith appearing, Judith disappearing, Judith staring out the window, Judith crooning those strange little tunes and talking to the trees as though they were listening?

Lynn opened the refrigerator door, took a piece of bread and stuffed it in her mouth to stop the stomach noises. She knew what she'd better do. Call Mouse.

"Mouse" was really Marjorie Beasley, but her nickname suited her better. Her hair was short and rather clipped off below the ears. She had a nose that sloped in the usual fashion and then tilted suddenly upward at the end, curving back around like the bottom of the letter *b*. Two small dark eyes peered out through enormous glasses. Marjorie was a month older than Lynn, but seemed younger because she was so short and skinny. No one would have guessed she was going into sixth grade in the fall.

Lynn sat down by the telephone in the front hall and dialed her number. "Mouse," she said, "I've got to talk to you."

"What about? I just woke up."

"I can't say. You'll have to come over."

"What have you got to eat?" Mouse asked, not particularly impressed.

"Just a minute and I'll look." Lynn laid down the phone and checked the refrigerator. Mouse always had to be bribed.

"Wheaties," she said, coming back. "And bananas

7

and Fritos and some ham salad for lunch. That's all I could find."

Mouse considered it. "I'll have breakfast here," she said. "Mom left some waffles. Be over later."

"Listen, Mouse, this is urgent! This is the most urgent thing I ever had to tell you!"

There was no reply. Maybe Marjorie had gone to sleep. Lynn whispered into the receiver. "This is about life and death and everything awful."

"I'll be over as soon as I eat my waffle," Mouse said and hung up.

Lynn made her way barefoot back through the kitchen again and onto the screened porch. Cereal and muffins sat waiting on the small table by the glider. Lynn poured some Wheaties in her bowl, rested it against her stomach, and leaned back to think over what she would tell Mouse.

Beyond the back porch was Mother's garden, separating the lawn from the big field. And beyond the field, with its brambles and blueberry bushes, ran Cowden's Creek, winding its way around the town and joining up somewhere with the Wabash. It ran deep in some places, shallow in others, and was nice for swimming if you didn't mind the crawfish.

There was really only one big hill in town, and the Morleys lived on it—not right at the top—that was Mrs. Tuggle's house—but on one side of it, where the street ran steep and wide. The sidewalks were of old brick,

laid at an angle, and oak trees lined the pavement a
down as Lindon's Corner, their heavy branches forn
a canopy of leaves in the summer and snow in
winter.

Like the Morleys', every house on the street had been
built with gables and porches and bay windows framed
in stained-glass insets. Yet each house was different
from all of the others. The Morleys', for instance, was
the only house with a closet under the stairs and an
attic above the third floor. Beneath the attic was one
great room divided by a heavy curtain. Lynn slept on
one side and Judith on the other. Lynn's part of the
room had the gables and faced the street; Judith's over-
looked the field in back. On the floor beneath were their
parents' bedroom, Stevie's, a bath, and a sewing room.
And on the first floor were the living and dining rooms
with their pillared doorways, the huge kitchen, and
a cozy little alcove called the music room because it
held a piano. The bay window was in the music room,
with a cushioned window seat—the favorite sitting–talking place for Lynn and Mouse. Beneath the whole
house, of course, was the basement with its earthen
floor, smelling of onions and potatoes and apples. It was
the only house Lynn ever remembered, having lived
there all her life.

She went back inside and put the milk in the refrigerator. With Mother gone, five-year-old Stevie asleep, and
Judith floating around somewhere above, the house had

an eerie kind of stillness, broken only by the occasional creaking and moaning of the old beams and floorboards.

Lynn climbed the stairs to the landing, the stairs to the second floor, and then the steep stairs to the third, which led right into her bedroom. Beyond the heavy drawn curtain, she could hear pages turning and knew that Judith was back there reading.

She stuck her pajamas in the drawer and pulled on her shorts and shirt. Then she brushed her hair and pulled it back into a ponytail, trying not to look in the mirror as she did so. Lynn didn't care for mirrors because she seldom liked what she saw—a somewhat long face with gray eyes and faint freckles on pale skin—absolutely nothing to get excited about. Not even a dimple.

A row of white daisies, growing in small pots, sat on the windowsill of Lynn's room. She studied them as she twisted a rubber band around her hair in back, and wondered what Judith was growing on her side of the room. *Hemlock*, she thought, pulling on her sneakers.

"Where are you going?" Judith's voice intruded so suddenly that Lynn jumped. How did Judith know she was going anywhere?

"Out. With Mouse."

"Don't forget to do your work before Mom comes home at lunchtime."

Lynn ran downstairs and checked the list on the closet door. Mom would have made a good army sergeant or a schoolteacher or a travel agent or something. She was full of ideas and plans, which she jotted down on paper and taped around the house. Time, she always said, was a priceless possession, and housework was for getting out of the way as quickly as possible.

Monday, read the list on the closet door. *Lynn: make beds, run carpet sweeper over downstairs rugs, do lunch dishes, keep an eye on Stevie in the afternoon.*

She grabbed the carpet sweeper from the closet, rolled it quickly over the rugs, and shoved it back inside just as Marjorie rang the bell.

Mouse lived two blocks away in a house with four gables instead of three. She arrived on her bike, which she always parked directly at the bottom of the long steps, making Mr. Morley boom, whenever he saw it, "Is that Beasley girl here again?"

Marjorie's father owned a store on First Avenue that sold rare books, her mother worked as a secretary in a dentist's office, and her two brothers were married, which meant that Mouse was more or less on her own during the summer. This probably explained why she dressed the way she did and why Judith seemed so repelled by her.

Clothes, to Marjorie Beasley, were a legal necessity having no useful function whatsoever except in wintertime. Shoes were obviously meant to come untied and trip her, socks to sag, jeans to rip, shirts to wrinkle and choke her about the neck, and if Marjorie owned a dress, Lynn was not sure she had ever seen it. Once, for a whole week, Mouse had come to school in a huge poncho that hung down below her bony knees, and Lynn had suspected she had nothing on underneath but a pair of pants. It certainly simplified dressing.

On this particular day, Mouse had on one yellow sock and one white one, a pair of sneakers that had ripped out at the toes, and the same jeans and shirt she had worn all week.

Lynn bolted through the screen. "Not here," she said. "We've got to go to our private place."

Mouse clattered down the porch steps after her, her glasses bobbing on her nose. "Wow! It must be super-secret!"

Lynn raced ahead, galloping down the long flight of stone steps to the sidewalk below. A moment later the girls were flying down the hill on Marjorie's bicycle, careening around the corner, and heading out the west road toward the cemetery.

Cemeteries were good talking places. There was a spot under an oak tree in the center where the tombstone of Mrs. Elfreda Lewis had fallen down in front of the tombstone of Mr. Lewis, making a perfect chair with a high back. Lynn always took this seat, while Mouse sat on a scroll held between two angels.

Sitting there on the scroll usually made Mouse quiet and rather pensive. The drama of death held a certain

fascination for her, and if she wasn't supposing how it felt to be dead and have no feeling, she was imagining she was being lifted right up to the sky by the white marble angels who looked sadly down upon her with no eyelids at all. But this time she couldn't wait for the news.

"What!" she whispered. "Tell me."

Lynn chose her words carefully. It was a terrible accusation she was making, and she had to say it just right. She sat up straight on the tombstone, folded her hands, and said evenly, "I've come to the conclusion that Judith possesses supernatural powers."

"What?"

"I suspect that she is being influenced by spirits and creatures of another realm."

"You mean? . . ."

"Exactly. Judith is a witch."

Mouse leaned forward, her arms around the angels' necks, and stared. "Lynn, are you sure?"

"Of course I'm not positive. I've got to have proof, and you've got to help me. But I sincerely, honestly, truthfully believe that she is."

"Why?"

Oh, it was delicious—too delicious, almost, to talk about. The goose bumps stood out on Lynn's arms just thinking about it.

"Dozens of things. Because of the way the tadpoles were swimming right over to her down at the creek.

Because of the way she sings to herself and talks to things and stares right through a person. It can happen, you know, to anybody. Spirits can take over anyone."

Mouse squirmed a little between the angels. A gusty breeze whipped over the graveyard, rustling the thick foliage of the oak trees above, contrasting sharply with the silence of the dead.

"But Lynn, it's got to be more than just tadpoles! You need more evidence than that."

"I know. Mouse, do you remember when I had poison ivy all over my legs and had to wear bandages to school? And Stevie got it on his arms? We were all picking daisies out in the field—Judith and Stevie and I—and Judith didn't get poison ivy at all. Doesn't that seem strange to you? And remember that awful storm on my birthday? And Judith had a gorgeous day for her party. And when our family went to Chicago during spring vacation, someone broke into the car and stole all our coats—all except Judith's raincoat. They left that right on the seat as if there was a hex on it or something. And Judith never even seems surprised. She *knows* it's going to happen, because she plans it that way. She reads books and she won't let me see them, and she sings strange songs—croons them, really. And you never hear her coming or going anymore. She just shows up some-where and the next minute she's gone."

Marjorie sat quietly a moment, thinking it over. "Is that all?" she asked finally.

"No." Lynn sat forward on her knees and faced Mouse. "I think she's in the power of someone else."

Mouse glanced at her sideways. "Who?" she asked warily.

"Somebody very old and wise . . ."

"Mrs. Tuggle?"

"Right. Judith's up there half the time, isn't she? Mrs. Tuggle's supposedly teaching her to sew, but Judith never brings home anything she's made and nobody asks any questions."

"How often does she go?"

"Several times a week. She stays for hours. And when she gets home, she goes right to her room and hums and recites little things to herself."

"Have you told your folks all this?"

"Not yet. I've got to be sure. But listen: not a single word to anyone. Promise! If it's true—and if Judith knows that we know—well . . . Mouse, have you ever heard of bodily transportation?"

"Body what?"

"A witch," Lynn told her, "can use her psychic powers to transport a person bodily from one place to another. If Judith even suspected we knew, she could put us down in Brazil. She'd tell Mom we got in a car with a stranger, and nobody would ever hear of us again."

Marjorie's nose wriggled with excitement. "What are we going to do, then?"

"I don't know. I haven't decided yet. But we'd better

learn all we can about witchcraft so we can stop her before she does something awful."

"Lynn, I know!" Mouse leaped off the scroll so suddenly that her glasses slipped and dangled from one ear.

"Know what?"

"Last week Daddy came home with a box of old books he bought at an auction. He said they were very valuable; and there was one on witchcraft. I know! He showed it to me. *Spells and Potions*. That was the name."

"Mouse, you've got to get it for me."

"I can't. Daddy said the books weren't to leave the house."

"Then there's only one thing left to do," Lynn said, looking right at her.

"I know," said Mouse miserably.

"Every word," added Lynn. "You've got to read every word, Mouse, so we don't miss anything."

"Lynn, there are four hundred pages!"

"But Mouse, it could mean my life."

"Okay, I'll do it." Marjorie sighed. "But all that reading's going to make me hungry."

"Peanut butter sandwiches. As many as you want. I'll make them myself."

Lynn got a ride back as far as the hill, where Mouse let her off and went on home. Slowly Lynn climbed the steep slope, walking pigeon-toed to fit her feet on the pattern of slanting brick.

It all made sense somehow. If anybody in the Morley family was prone to possession, it was Judith. Judith, unlike herself, was a follower, Lynn decided. Weren't the walls of Judith's room covered with pictures of famous actors and singing stars? Didn't she always have to wear whatever shoes or jeans or earrings the other girls were wearing? Didn't Judith study her astrology guide every day and believe whatever the horoscope told her?

Since she had been spending her evenings at Mrs. Tuggle's, however, Judith had spent less and less time with her girl friends. She had stopped listening to rock and hummed instead the wisps of tunes she'd learned from Mrs. Tuggle. She was slowly changing, and nobody seemed to notice. Except her, Lynn. For some reason, she was able to see things more clearly than she ever had before, and she did not like what she saw in Judith.

She reached the house and walked up the long flight of steps to the walk above, then up the steps to the porch. Even before she opened the screen, she heard the strange crooning. Cautiously, she slipped inside.

Judith was sitting on the window seat in the music room. She was dressed in blue shorts and a blue shirt, and her long dark hair hung loosely down her back and over her shoulders. Her face was like a delicate china doll's, with perfectly formed lips. Judith was slightly on the plump side, but Lynn would have traded figures

18

with her instantly if only she could have had her sister's face in the bargain.

Judith was sitting very still, and her eyes had a far-away look in them, as though she were still half-asleep. Then Lynn noticed that she was holding a jar in her hands, turning it absently around and around in the sunlight, and chanting softly:

> *From the shadows of the pool,*
> *Black as midnight, thick as gruel,*
> *Come, my nymphs, and you shall be*
> *Silent images of me.*

Judith's fingernails seemed unusually long, Lynn thought—longer than she'd ever noticed before. Judith

was staring into the jar with strange fascination as she crooned, and suddenly Lynn's heart leaped up. There were tadpoles in the jar, and Judith was talking to them as though they were in her control—as though she had the power to change them into something else.

"Where did you go?" came Judith's voice. She didn't even turn around. Lynn was sure she hadn't made a sound.

"How did you know I was back?"

"Why are you always spying on me?" Judith asked in answer.

Lynn shrugged, trying to sound casual. "Who's interested in you? Just didn't think you heard me come in, that's all." She stood there a moment watching her sister and suddenly felt a twinge of concern. "Judith, why don't you go out somewhere? It's better than sitting around all day by yourself."

Judith's lips turned into a strange kind of smile, and she bent over her jar again, watching the tadpoles with an odd kind of tenderness. "Maybe I have friends you don't even know about," she said, almost to herself, and Lynn fled silently upstairs.

chapter two

Mrs. Morley came home for lunch with the announcement that her studio was in order, the books in their proper places, the envelopes and paper, stamps, erasers, and carbons arranged just so, and there was no reason on earth why she couldn't get to work on her half-written book immediately. Whenever Mother said there was no reason on earth, it meant she was having trouble with the plot.

Stevie was up now, eating a bowl of Sugar Crisps. He looked a little like Mother. Both their faces were round, and their blue eyes were spaced wide apart. Lynn was the only one who looked like her father, and that's why she never cared for mirrors. Not that Father was ugly. His looks went well on him, but they weren't so great on a girl.

"Why don't you write a book about dinosaurs?" Stevie asked, burrowing his spoon down deep in the cereal and filling his mouth to overflowing.

"Because I don't know any dinosaurs," Mrs. Morley said matter-of-factly. She was putting a new shoelace in Stevie's sneaker between bites of her sandwich. "As soon as I write about something I don't know anything about, something I can scarcely even imagine, I know right away that the book can't be any good. If I wrote a story about a dinosaur, it would look like a dog, behave like a horse, and have a boy's name, and who would believe a dinosaur like that?"

"Write about that time when you were a girl and got lost in Milwaukee," Lynn suggested.

But Mrs. Morley shook her head. "That's just not the way an idea comes. It's nothing anyone can give me. It has to start inside my own head. I have to stumble on it myself and know that it's meant for me. Right now I have little wisps of things in my mind—little fragments of a story that hasn't put itself together yet— pages that are all disconnected. It will come, but sometimes it's hard waiting."

"I'm sure not going to be an author and write in a hen house," Judith said from her chair on the back porch where she was eating alone. "I want to be something really different . . . haunting . . . something dreamy. . . ."

"There aren't too many opportunities to be dreamy, my dear," Mrs. Morley told her, putting Stevie's shoe on for him and tying it. "No matter what you decide to be, it's going to have its gringy moments." She got up and gave her brown hair a quick combing in the mirror over the sink. "Okay, I'm off. See you around four." She started outside, then stuck her head back in. "I got a new shovel for you, Stevie. It's on the back porch."

Stevie went out to play in the sand at the side of the house, and Lynn watched him for a while from the window seat in the music room. The baby fat on his chubby legs dimpled as he squatted there in the sand, his lips puckered as he worked at digging a tunnel for his trucks. Lynn could remember when Judith had enjoyed playing with him. Now she was all wrapped up in herself.

The phone rang, and it was Mouse. Lynn sprawled on the cool oak floor in the hallway, the receiver to her ear.

"What's up?" she asked.

"Chapter one, page seven;" came Marjorie's voice over the wire. " 'The ability of witches to perform tremendous feats is a result of their combined psychic efforts when gathered together as a coven; this is called raising the cone of power. Though the traditional number is seven, a group consisting of no more than two or three sometimes considers itself a coven.' "

Mouse stopped for breath, and Lynn took over. "You see, Mouse!" she whispered. "If a witch has even one more person to work with, her power is stronger!"

"Right. Page ten: 'In the sixteenth century, witches rubbed their bodies with an ointment made of thorn apples, belladonna, parsley, and the fat of an un-baptized infant.' "

Lynn gasped.

". . . 'They have also been accused of making pacts with the devil and riding on broomsticks greased with boiled-down babies.' "

There was the sound of Stevie's crying outside, punc-tuated by little shrieks.

"Just a minute, Mouse," Lynn said and raced to the back door. Judith was coming across the yard holding Stevie by one arm.

"Will you please keep him home?" Judith said to Lynn. "He's your responsibility for this afternoon, and I don't want him following me around."

"I wanna go swimming too!" Stevie wailed. "Judith's going, and I wanna swim too."

"Wait till I get through talking with Mouse and I'll take you down to the creek," Lynn promised, noting the red marks on his arm where Judith had squeezed it. They did not look like ordinary marks, somehow, but had the appearance of scratches made by claws.

"Please just wait till I'm through!" Judith demanded. "Can't I ever have a little privacy?" She turned and flounced back across the lawn, through Mother's garden, and out into the field toward Cowden's Creek, beach towel flapping over her arm.

"Come on in the kitchen and I'll give you a glass of Kool-Aid," Lynn said. "We'll go swimming later when Judith gets back."

When Stevie had calmed down, Lynn went back to the telephone.

"It was Stevie and Judith," she said uneasily.

"I know," Mouse told her. "I could hear Judith yelling. Listen, Lynn. I've got to ask: Is Stevie baptized?"

"I don't know," Lynn said. "He . . . oh, no!"

"The fat of an unbaptized infant, but maybe it doesn't matter if the fat is five years old."

"Oh, Mouse! She wouldn't!" Lynn declared. "I mean, I know he gets in her way and everything, but . . ."

"Okay, it was just an idea. I'm going to start chapter two now. See you later."

An hour later Judith came back from the creek. She brushed past Lynn and slowly ascended the stairs to her room on the third floor, crooning her strange little tune. Lynn broke out in goose pimples, and when she looked down, she saw the same marks on her own arm she had seen on Stevie's.

Mrs. Morley had been in the hen house for one week and hadn't written so much as a paragraph that she hadn't crossed out later.

"I don't know what's the matter," she said one evening. "I just can't latch hold of the plot. I think I've got it, and then it's gone again. Nothing hangs together." She was trying to braid Lynn's hair in a fancy style that hung down her back, but Lynn doubted it would make her beautiful.

Father moved the rook on the chessboard in front of him and studied the position for a while. His long fingers rested lightly on the piece, and his narrow face widened in a smile. "Seems like the moment you moved in the hen house, you laid an egg," he quipped.

"I don't find that amusing, Richard," Mother said. Whenever she called Father "Richard," she was really upset.

"I know, sweetheart, but you'll have to admit you work in rather odd surroundings."

"They're perfectly fine surroundings! The studio is comfortable and convenient, and I wish you would all stop harassing me about it! When you have problems with your work, do I tell you to get yourself another office?"

"No, can't say that you do."

"Then let's face it—the trouble is *me*!" Mother vigorously brushed out the braid and tried something else. Lynn sat still, enjoying it. "I stare at the typewriter and it stares back at me, and the paper just sits there going nowhere. Maybe I wasn't meant to be a writer," she said darkly. "Maybe I ought to do something else."

"I think you're working too hard at it," Father suggested. "You ought to forget about it awhile and just let

26

it come spontaneously. This isn't the first time you've hit a block, you know, but you always seem to pull through." He moved a piece on the chessboard. "Check," he said to himself, and rested his chin in his hands. Mother's nimble fingers piled Lynn's hair high on her head, with two curls on either side, and handed her the mirror. *Not bad*, Lynn thought, pleased.

"I could turn that hen house into a bakery and sell muffins, pies, and cobblers. And I could publish recipe books and historical notes about Indiana. What do you think, Dick?"

"I think it makes a nice pipe dream till you get your new book going again," said Father.

"*I* think it's a *great* idea!" Stevie put in from the dining room where he was building a Tinker Toy masterpiece.

"Oh, Mother, you always say that," Lynn reminded her. "When I was seven years old, you said if you couldn't write, you'd sell homemade bread. Remember?"

Mr. Morley swooped one big hand over the board, confiscated all the pieces, and set up a new chess problem. "Lynn, you ought to know by now that your mother isn't happy unless she's creating something. Before she even started creating children, she was creating books, and if the well ever runs dry, you can bet she'll be creating something else."

"Please don't refer to my head as a well," Mother said.

"You'll have me worrying about a water shortage."

Mr. Morley grinned. "You know that'll never happen, Sylvia. Writing's in your blood. I knew that when I married you. You're never happier and nicer to be around than when you're deep in a story and it's going fine."

"And when it's not, and the ideas won't come? . . ."

"Exactly."

"All right," Mother promised. "I'll not even think about the book for a few days. I'll go make a blueberry cobbler instead."

"I wanna help with the crust!" Stevie said, and danced out to the kitchen behind her.

"Dad," Lynn asked, holding her head very still so the curls wouldn't fall down, "is Stevie baptized?"

Mr. Morley didn't even look up. "No. Our church doesn't do things that way. We dedicate children, but we don't baptize them. Why?"

"Just wondering," Lynn said. She just wished Stevie didn't have so much baby fat, that's all.

There was a picnic on the weekend, and Mrs. Morley abandoned herself to the joy of the moment. If she thought about her book, she didn't show it, and Lynn especially enjoyed these close times with her mother. Like mountain goats, the Morleys climbed single file up the steep trails of the state park, pointing out sights below and yelping with delight whenever they spotted a nest or a snake or a jack rabbit hurling itself over the brambles. Even Judith snapped out of her lethargy for the day, and smiled at Father's teasing, as though getting away from the neighborhood broke the spell somehow.

"What's the matter, Judith? Got lead in your boots?" Mr. Morley asked as she dragged behind, exhausted from the long climb up to the lookout point.

"It's not fair!" Judith said laughing. "You and Lynn have the only long legs in the family. I have to take two steps for every one of yours!"

Lynn couldn't believe it. Judith actually envied something of hers. It gave Lynn a warm feeling of closeness toward her sister. Judith was even thoughtful.

"One marshmallow left, Lynn. You want it?" she asked as she toasted the last in the sack.

"Sure. Any time!" Lynn said.

And when the marshmallows were gone and the lunch had been cleared away, Judith took Stevie over to the swings and swung a long time with him on her lap.

"Oh, what a marvelous day!" Mother said, walking back to the car with her arm around Lynn, the wind blowing her hair about her face. "I feel utterly uncrinkled. Let's do this again before the summer's over."

They rode back home, Stevie in the front seat beside his father, and Mrs. Morley in back with the girls. Lynn started, "White Coral Bells," and Mother and Judith joined in. Then they did "Row, Row, Row Your Boat" and all the other rounds they could think of.

Sitting there beside Judith, Lynn felt she'd probably been very wrong about her sister. Maybe now she was going to be friendly the way she used to be, when they would lie in bed talking long after the lights were out, and Judith would tell all her secrets. But as soon as they reached home, as soon as Judith started up the steps, in fact, the mood came over her again. She went up to her room and drew the curtain, and when Lynn asked if she could come in, Judith said no, she was reading. There was no sound of pages turning, however, and as Lynn lay in her bed on the other side of the curtain, almost asleep, she thought she heard the faint tinkle of a bell. Or perhaps it was only Judith's wind chime.

On Monday evening, Judith left earlier than usual for Mrs. Tuggle's, and Lynn realized how little she herself had seen of the old woman. What she had seen, however, she remembered surprisingly well; somehow she seemed to have an accurate memory for storing away odds and ends, and she had only to close her eyes to picture Mrs. Tuggle vividly.

She was a short woman, an inch shorter than Judith, with a frail, little body and bony shoulders that protruded up under the sleeves of her dress like two metal doorknobs. Her hair was gray and wound into a small tight bun at the back of her head, but her eyebrows were dark black, as though they had been taken from another face and pasted above her eyes. There was something about Mrs. Tuggle's large jaws, however, that gave her a look of strength, as though hidden inside the small, frail woman was a person of unusual power.

She had come to Indiana years ago from Castletown in England, and though she had long since given up tea and biscuits in the late afternoon, she still spoke with a lilting British accent. The few times Lynn had visited her, Mrs. Tuggle's talk had soon turned to the thatch-roofed cottages and hedgerows she loved so much, to haunted castles and fog above the cliffs, and to ghosts that roamed the moors.

"Just her way of whiling away the long winter evenings," Mother always said of her stories. "And anyway, aren't they marvelous? And the little verses she knows!"

But the more Lynn thought about it that night, the clearer it all became. Wasn't it about the time that Judith began going to Mrs. Tuggle's that her strangeness began? Wasn't that about the time the girls were making fudge, and Lynn's burned, but Judith's didn't? That Lynn got the twenty-four-hour flu, but Judith didn't? That Lynn had three cavities and Judith, for the first time, had none? Wouldn't such tricks as these be appropriate for a beginning witch?

Who really knew very much about the little woman high on the hill in the oldest house of all? Wasn't it

Mrs. Tuggle herself who had suggested that Mother use her hen house as a studio, that Judith come by for sewing lessons? Maybe Mrs. Tuggle was spinning her web, and Judith had been the first to get trapped.

"What does Judith *do* there all that time?" Lynn asked her mother.

"She's making a wardrobe for school. Mrs. Tuggle is an excellent seamstress, and it will be wonderful if Judith learns to sew as well as she does. Besides, Mrs. Tuggle's lonely. It's good for her to have a young girl about, and she and Judith seem to get along nicely together."

It was obvious that Mother suspected nothing.

"Mouse," Lynn said over the phone on Tuesday, "can you come by this evening?"

"Sure!"

"Leave your bike at home, and come about eight. I'll tell you the rest later."

"Right."

The afternoon ticked slowly by. Judith washed her hair and lay out in a sunny place on the porch to let it dry. Lynn sat down on the glider at the other end and watched her. She had to be careful. Very careful.

"Going to Mrs. Tuggle's tonight?" Lynn asked innocently, flipping through a magazine.

Judith opened her eyes and closed them again. "I suppose."

"What do you do there so long?" Lynn quizzed. "You

could have made ten skirts and a dozen blouses by now."

"I'm making a pants suit," Judith replied, "and it's hard to fit. I have to rip out half of what I make. Sometimes Mrs. Tuggle recites poetry, or else we just talk."

Lynn tried not to sound too curious. "What about?"

"Cabbages and kings," Judith retorted. "Now let me enjoy the quiet, please, while Stevie is out. It's like a boiler factory when he's around."

Dinner came and went. Judith disappeared behind the thick curtain dividing the girls' room and emerged some time later with her blue satin box—her sewing box, she said, but no one had ever seen inside it.

"Going to Mrs. Tuggle's, Mother," she called, pulling on her sandals, and when Lynn turned around, she was gone. The screen didn't even slam. Like the Wicked Witch of the East, she pulled on her slippers and simply disappeared.

At eight, Lynn met Marjorie coming up from the walk below.

"You know what we've got to do tonight, Mouse? Spy on Mrs. Tuggle and Judith and see what really goes on."

"Ye gods," said Mouse, and sat down on the steps. "You should have told me."

"Why? What difference would it make?"

"I'd be prepared."

"How?"

"I'd have stayed home, that's what."

Lynn sat down beside her. "Well, we can't go yet. Let's wait till it gets a little darker." She hugged herself with her arms and was surprised to discover she was shivering. "How do they do it, anyway, Mouse? How do witches make spells and everything?"

"I'm just getting to that part." Mouse pushed back her big glasses, which kept slipping down her nose. "There are all kinds of ways. Sometimes they make sort of a doll to look like someone in particular. Then they stick pins in it and recite special words, and pretty soon the person gets sick. That's one way. Or they write the spells on a piece of paper, burn it in the flame of a candle, and keep the ashes."

"I'll bet Judith's memorized them all by this time," Lynn said. She was quiet awhile. "Mouse," she said finally, "can you imagine yourself getting involved in something like that? I mean, someone talking you into witchcraft?"

"Sure. Easy."

"How come?"

"Because I'm a coward," Mouse said simply. "All Mrs. Tuggle would have to do is look at me cross-eyed and I'd be chanting hexes. I've absolutely no backbone."

"I don't believe it. It wouldn't happen unless you wanted it to."

"So maybe Judith wants it. Maybe witchcraft's her career. I mean, don't knock it till you've tried it."

"Oh, for goodness' sake, Mouse, I've got better plans

than that."

"Like what?"

Lynn wasn't really sure what she wanted to be. She was only sure of what she didn't want. She *didn't* want to be under the thumb of someone else. She wanted control over her own life. She was nobody's follower. But she was also intensely curious about other people and the choices they made. She had to know why.

"Maybe I'll be a psychiatrist," she ventured.

"Then I'll be your first patient," said Mouse.

The Tuggle house sat at the very top of the hill, surrounded by an empty lot on each side, which Mr. Tuggle had farmed when he was alive. Tall trees cast their shadows on the house, and a thorn apple hid the front door completely from view. In the vast yard behind, which sloped directly down to the creek, were an old barn, a tractor shed, and the hen house.

As the girls made their way up the brick sidewalk along the street, the house stood out starkly against the purple sky, its turrets and gables more fancy and numerous than any other house on the street—a gingerbread house with nothing sweet about it.

There was only one light burning besides the one in the hall—a light in a second-floor window. An upper porch extended around three sides of the house like a balcony, with a staircase leading down to the side yard.

"We're going up," Lynn whispered in the gathering

darkness, and slowly, one foot over the other, they started up, edging forward uncertainly, as though one false step would bring the porch down upon them. Each time the ancient steps creaked, the girls froze in their tracks, one foot suspended, and then, when there was no response from inside, they went on.

The porch itself listed slightly toward the street, and as Lynn moved around it, she felt as if she were on a huge, silent ship, tipping slowly into the sea. Breathing short breaths, lips apart, she clutched Marjorie's sleeve, heart pounding, and they inched their way to the lighted window where they could see Judith and Mrs. Tuggle inside.

The old woman sat in a chair by the table with a garment across her lap. Swiftly her fingers moved along the hem, pushing and plucking at the needle in rapid succession, like a woman born in a fitting room and reared amid great bolts of cloth. She was talking to Judith, but so softly that Lynn could not understand her words. Judith was listening in rapt attention, hypnotized, it seemed, by the sound of the voice. And then, as Lynn watched, Judith's fingers slowly opened the blue box, lifted out a small doll in a red plaid skirt, and plunged a pin through the top of the skirt, deep in the soft body of the doll.

"Mouse!" Lynn breathed, too horrified to say more. Wildly the girls clung to each other there in the darkness, for another pin went into the doll and still another.

Slowly Judith turned the doll around and around, stabbing it with pins. Then she handed the doll to Mrs. Tuggle and stood up.

Moving swiftly backward, away from the window, the girls fled to the top of the stairs on silent feet, tiptoed down, and ran, with hearts racing, across the empty lot, flinging themselves over bushes and flower beds until they collapsed, panting, on the grass outside the Morleys' back porch.

Judith didn't come home till after nine. But at ten that evening the phone rang, and when Lynn answered, she heard Marjorie's weak voice saying, "Lynn! I've got an awful stomachache! How about you?"

chapter three

So the pins had been meant for Marjorie! Lynn woke early the next morning and lay in bed staring through the row of daisies that lined her window. It was an unusually hot day, so it felt good not to move. Her mind went back to the night before. She had always known that Judith didn't care much for Mouse.

"She's so sloppy I don't see how her own mother can stand her," Judith had said once. "And that laugh of hers! Does she have to go around squeaking like that?"

"I don't make fun of your friends," Lynn had retorted.

"Oh, I'm not making fun of her," Judith said. "But for heaven's sake don't invite her over when I've got company, that's all."

Behind the curtain in the center of the large room, Lynn could hear Judith's breathing, and it made her angry. Mouse had probably been up half the night with a stomachache, and Judith slept as though she had nothing whatever to do with it.

For a moment Lynn felt like storming through the curtain, waking Judith up, and demanding to know why she'd done it. But she knew how foolish that would be.

She got out of bed and tiptoed across the floor. How long had it been since she'd gone in Judith's room, anyway? Weeks. Judith had to pass through Lynn's room to get downstairs, but there was no occasion for anyone to go into hers. In fact, the family had been forbidden.

"It's *my* room, and I'll clean it myself," Judith had told Mother. "I want a place that's private, some place I can really call my own."

Well, perhaps it was time somebody took a look. Carefully, Lynn pulled the thick curtain aside. The sunlight from her own window fell on Judith's face, and she looked almost angelic lying there with one arm thrown over the edge of the bed.

Lynn's heart beat rapidly as she glanced about the room. She half expected to see bats hanging from the ceiling and a tall pointed hat on the bedpost. The room, however, looked as if it might belong to any fourteen-year-old girl, except for two items: a broom in one corner, and a candle on the dresser.

"What are you doing?"

Judith rose straight up in bed so suddenly that Lynn jumped. Before she could answer, Judith said, "You're spying, obviously. I told you to stay out."

"I—I just wanted to make sure your windows were open," Lynn stammered. "I got too warm."

"They're always open." Judith lay back down and turned over.

"Anyway, I couldn't sleep," Lynn added. "I was worrying about Mouse. She was terribly sick last night."

Judith's eyes opened again. "What was wrong with her?"

"A bad stomachache." Lynn watched her sister closely.

"Probably all that junk she eats," Judith commented. "She eats all the time. Now will you please get out and let me sleep?"

When the mail was delivered that morning, there was an airmail letter for Mrs. Morley, and Lynn decided to take it to her. There was no phone in the hen house to distract Mother while she wrote, and she had asked that someone run up the hill with her mail any time she got something that looked important. It was exactly the opportunity Lynn needed.

Mrs. Tuggle's house looked no better by daylight. In fact, its need for paint was even more obvious. But there were no banging shutters or hanging doors or cobwebs stretched across broken windows. From the outside it simply looked like the house of an old woman who didn't quite keep it up the way she used to.

There was an old brick walk, half covered with moss, that led to the barn behind the house, branching off at one point toward the hen house. Lynn found herself standing outside a small building with a low roof, the windows clustered on each end. There was a little stove-pipe chimney sticking out the top, and the door had been painted a rusty orange. Strange as it seemed, with her own mother inside, she still felt it proper to knock first.

"Good! A visitor!" Mother said cheerfully, opening the screen. "Come in and see what I've done to the hen house."

Lynn stepped inside and stared. Mother had been busy. The frames around each window were orange like the door, and there was a round braided rug of orange, white, and yellow on the cement floor. The entire back wall, completely covered with built-in boxes where the hens had once nested, now held all manner of writing supplies: large envelopes in one, small envelopes in another, manila envelopes, carbon sets, bond paper, second sheets, reference books, published books, old manuscripts, file folders—each of them had a special place. Mother's big desk sat at one end under the windows, and a rocking chair perched cozily by the old coal stove, waiting for winter. There were two file cabinets in one corner, plus a few boxes of unsorted odds and ends.

"Oh, Mother!" Lynn said admiringly.

"Isn't it exquisite?" Mrs. Morley burbled. "I wanted to wait till I had the curtains up before I let anyone see it, but we'll just consider this a preview. And to think I get it for only fifteen dollars a month, plus electricity! Of course, I have to bring my own water in a thermos, and if I need a bathroom, I have to use Mrs. Tuggle's, but it's a studio of my own, way back here where it's quiet and private." She sat down at her desk and opened the letter. "I was making myself a cup of tea on the hot plate before the day gets too warm. Why don't you stay and have some with me?"

It was exactly what Lynn had hoped she would say, so she sat down in the rocker and waited. She felt very adult, somehow, having tea with an author in her studio, and never mind that it was her own mother.

"Well!" Mrs. Morley said, staring at the letter in her hand. "Guess what? A writers' conference in Illinois wants me to give a lecture next month—all expenses paid. I'm supposed to talk about writing children's books. Isn't that exciting?"

"You mean you'll be going away?" Lynn asked, somewhat uneasily.

"Only for a weekend. This is the first time I've been asked. I think I'll celebrate and put a lump of sugar in my tea!"

She looked like a schoolgirl, Lynn decided, puttering about the hot plate there on the file cabinet, her brown hair pulled back with a green scarf. She was barefoot because she always took her shoes off when she wrote. "It ventilates the brain," she said, and Father thought that exceptionally funny.

"I feel great today," Mother was saying, "even though I haven't accomplished a thing. Maybe that's a good sign." She poured the boiling water into two paper cups, added sugar and a tea bag, and handed one to Lynn. "It's hot, dear. Be careful." Then she sat down on the rug to drink it, legs stretched out in front of her, ankles crossed. "Well, how are things at home?"

How should she begin, Lynn wondered. She wished they had been talking of spirits or something so she could work it in naturally. Somehow the whole thing seemed too unbelievable for words, and Lynn was afraid it would all sound corny.

"Hmmmm?" Mother asked, watching her.

Lynn shrugged. "Oh, so-so. Sort of strange, I guess."

"Strange?"

Lynn turned her cup around and around in her hands. It seemed very odd talking with Mother like this, as though she were someone outside the family. If they were home, Mother would be bustling about the kitchen as they talked. Here in the studio, Lynn had her undivided attention.

"Mother," she said finally, "has anyone in our family ever been a witch . . . an aunt or somebody?"

Mrs. Morley looked puzzled. "Not that I know of."

"Do you believe in witches?"

"That's hard to say. I'm not sure how to answer."

"Well . . ." Lynn took a deep breath. "I've suspected for a long time that Judith is a witch." She looked straight at her mother, expecting her to laugh, but the same puzzled expression showed on Mrs. Morley's face.

"Judith? Why do you think so?"

It was easier now. Lynn put down the tea, not really wanting it, and leaned forward.

"Mother, there are all kinds of reasons—all kinds of strange things happening. You just don't know!"

"Well, let's hear some of them."

"For months Judith has been acting very odd. Haven't you noticed? She always wants to be alone, and she doesn't want anybody looking at her."

"But Lynn, Judith is growing up. She was just fourteen, and girls change a lot at that age. They're moody and dreamy, and keep all sorts of things to themselves. That's just the way they are."

"Not the way Judith is. I've seen her do . . . spooky things."

"Yes?"

"One day I was watching her down at the creek, and she was humming and the tadpoles swam right into her hands, just like she was calling them. And the way things are happening to everybody else and not to her. Like Stevie and me getting poison ivy and Judith not. And I got the flu and cavities, and Judith didn't. And that time in Chicago someone broke into the car and stole all our coats except Judith's."

Mrs. Morley leaned back against her desk. "Look, Lynn, it's natural for a younger sister to be a little bit jealous of someone who's older, and sometimes it does seem as though everything good comes her way, but I'm sure it's only coincidence."

"I'm not jealous, and it's not coincidence!" Lynn said hotly. "What happened last night was the worst yet."

Mrs. Morley stopped drinking her tea. "What happened?"

"Mouse and I . . . saw her . . . sticking pins in a doll. And later Mouse got a horrible stomachache." Somehow Lynn couldn't bring herself to mention Mrs. Tuggle. If she did, she might blow the whole thing, and Mother would never believe her. Convince her of Judith's witchcraft first and then tell her about the old woman, that was the sensible way.

Mrs. Morley drew up her knees and wrapped her arms around them, studying Lynn. She was not laughing. "You certainly have been very observant of your sister the last few months, Lynn. I had no idea all this was going on."

She believed! Lynn slid off the rocker and sat down on the rug near her.

"We've got to do something about it, Mother, before she does something to Stevie!" she said earnestly.

"Stevie?"

"Yes. Because he's not baptized."

"What?"

"Look. Mouse and I got this book, and it tells all the secrets of witchcraft and everything." Lynn was talking so fast she stumbled over her words. "Witches grease their broomsticks with the fat of unbaptized babies, and Judith has a broom in her room, and maybe Stevie's all she can get. And the marks she makes on his skin, Mother—like claw marks. They're not natural!"

"Lynn!" There was a firmness in her mother's voice now. "You are an intelligent girl, but you also have a very active imagination. Things might seem pretty suspicious if you're looking for trouble, but undoubtedly there are

47

good explanations for everything. It's quite possible that you and Marjorie are unconsciously making daily events support what you want to believe, which is that Judith is up to witchcraft. That doll you mentioned is probably her styling manikin. The scratches are undoubtedly from those long fingernails she's been growing. If you really wrote down everything that happened, you'd see that as many unpleasant things happen to Judith as to anybody else."

She didn't believe after all. Lynn felt the bottom drop out of her stomach. It was worse to have told Mother everything and find out she didn't believe it than not to have told her at all.

"Mother," she said, in a last desperate attempt to persuade her, "have I ever imagined that something actually happened when it didn't? Have I ever told you something that wasn't true?"

Mrs. Morley looked at her thoughtfully, carefully studying her face. "No, Lynn, you haven't. I'll admit that despite your imagination, you are a pretty accurate observer of people, and you sometimes seem to sense what they are thinking and feeling before anyone else. That's something I've always noticed about you. But in this case, I think you are coming to the wrong conclusions about things you have accurately observed. You're wrong, I'm sure, in concluding that any of this is witchcraft."

There was nothing left to argue, nothing more to say.

Finally Lynn muttered, "I don't think Judith should be taking care of Stevie. If anything happens to him, don't say I didn't warn you."

Mrs. Morley chuckled. She reached out and pulled Lynn to her, encircling her with one arm. "Judith is a very capable baby-sitter, my dear, and if I didn't think I could trust her, I wouldn't leave her in charge of the house while I'm working. It's a serious accusation, you know, calling somebody a witch."

Lynn pushed away. "You won't say anything to Judith, will you?"

"That I can promise," Mother said. "But why don't you go have a talk with her yourself? Ask her about some of the things you've told me—like the tadpoles. See what she says. Maybe she can explain it."

"Maybe," said Lynn, knowing she wouldn't ask. She got up. "Well, see you at lunchtime."

Lynn went outside and closed the screen. Mother was right about her imagination. Lynn had a way of "putting herself in another's skin," as Father called it. Sometimes when she lay in bed at night, she would imagine what it would be like to be trapped on the sixteenth floor of a hotel and have a choice of jumping or burning to death. Or to have her foot caught on a railroad track and hear a train whistle in the distance. Or to be a famous singer and forget the words in the middle of the song. By just thinking about it, Lynn could feel the flames or the terror or the panic and embarrassment.

Her heart would pound and her palms would perspire and her neck would feel all creepy in back. Sometimes she even moaned. She was sure that she actually *knew* what such an experience would be like. But never, ever, in 'all her life, had Lynn imagined that things were actually happening when they really weren't. There was a difference between being sensitive and being crazy.

She took a few steps up the walk and stopped. Through the windows she could see her mother. She was still on the rug in the same position Lynn had left her, her arms around her knees, and there was a faraway look on her face, as though she were completely absorbed in her thoughts. Maybe she did believe after all and just didn't want to alarm Lynn. Maybe she had known about it all the time and had moved her studio here so she could keep a closer eye on Mrs. Tuggle.

Nevertheless, Lynn felt uneasy. She was afraid that Judith would know she had talked to Mother. Or perhaps Mrs. Tuggle had seen her coming and guessed. And when she reached home, she was sure of it, because the daisies on her windowsill were dead—all of them. They hung limp and dry over the sides of their pots in the warm noon sun.

As soon as she could, she called Marjorie.

"How you feeling, Mouse?"

"Better, I guess." Her voice sounded faint. "Mom had to call the doctor. I was upchucking everything."

"What did he say?"

"He called it a 'green-apple stomach,' except that I haven't had any green apples. And he gave me some medicine and said to stay home today. What do you suppose Judith has against me, Lynn?"

"I don't know, Mouse. But it's not just you. All my daisies are dead, and they were okay this morning." Lynn was surprised to discover that her voice was shaking.

"Well, I know one thing. We've got to get that doll away from her before she tries something else. Boy, was I ever sick!"

"You mean . . . steal the doll?"

"That's exactly what I mean."

Lynn was quiet for a moment. Mouse sure didn't sound like a coward. "Okay," she said, taking a deep breath. "Meet me in the cemetery tomorrow afternoon, and we'll make plans. One o'clock."

A little later Lynn was dusting the buffet in the dining room, when she heard Judith getting out the bucket to scrub the kitchen floor, the work assigned for the day.

"I wish I had somethin' to do," came Stevie's voice from the kitchen doorway.

"Go build something with your blocks," Judith suggested.

"No," Stevie bellowed. "I'm tired of blocks. I want somethin' else."

"Play in the sand, then."

51

"I'm tired of sand."

"Then go find a friend. Don't just hang around griping," Judith answered, somewhat irritably. "I've got plenty to do."

"What?"

"I've got to scrub the kitchen floor."

"I wanna help."

"No. You'd just make a mess."

From the dining room doorway, Lynn could see Stevie taking off his shoes and socks, and a moment later, when Judith's back was turned, he waded across the wet floor, dipped a towel in the bucket, and began flinging it around over the linoleum.

"Cut that out!" Judith demanded. "You're slopping it all over the place!"

"You always get all the fun things to do, and I don't get any!" Stevie wailed.

"Oh, go drop!" Judith snapped. "Just get out of here."

Stevie padded back out and through the hall, leaving wet footprints on the oak floor. The screen slammed. There was a pause, a thud, and then a scream.

Lynn dashed to the front door to find that Stevie had fallen off the porch and down the steps. His lip was cut and there was blood on his shirt.

Go drop, Judith had said, and it had happened.

chapter four

The fallen tombstone of Mrs. Elfreda Lewis felt wonderfully cool on the back of Lynn's legs. She leaned against the tombstone of Mr. Lewis and looked up at Mouse, who was perched between the two angels, her arms draped affectionately around the neck of one.

"When I die," said Marjorie dreamily, "I want a big angel sort of bending over my grave with a flower in her hand and marble tears running down her cheeks."

Mouse was wearing a pair of jeans, torn at both knees, and an enormous purple T-shirt that hung far below the hips. She looked like an orphan just picked up off the streets by two heavenly visitors.

Lynn let her dream on for a while longer and then

reminded her of the purpose of their meeting.

"Who's going to get the doll?" she asked. "You or me?"

"You," Mouse replied instantly. "One bad stomachache is enough."

"It probably won't make any difference," Lynn mused. "She's getting to the point where she can cast spells even without the doll. Yesterday Stevie made her angry, and she told him to 'go drop.' He walked right off the porch and cut his lip as if he'd been hypnotized or something."

"Maybe if you *know* somebody is likely to put a hex on you, you can resist it," Mouse said. "Maybe if you lit a candle and held it under your chin and said, 'Hex, be gone,' seven times, it couldn't hurt you."

"Did you read that somewhere?"

"No," Mouse replied dolefully. "I made it up."

"The problem," said Lynn, "is that Judith is way ahead of us. She knows all kinds of things that we don't. Do you know what I saw in her room the other morning? A broom and a candle. Doesn't that seem odd to you?"

Marjorie slipped off the angels' scroll and crouched down beside Lynn. "What color was the candle? It wasn't black, was it? Or red?"

"I . . . I think it was purple."

Mouse sucked in her breath. "I read about candles last night. Chapter Five. Purple is for contacting the spirits. And if you ring a small clear bell nine times or let a teakettle whistle, it will bring visitors from the other world. Does she have a bell?"

"I don't know. I haven't seen one, but I thought I heard one the other night just as I was falling asleep."

"Does she have any rings?"

"She used to, but she never wears them."

Mouse's face was drawn up in a serious scowl. "Lynn, have you ever heard of the full-moon ring spell?"

"No . . ."

"The full-moon ring is one of the first spells a witch casts, because it protects her. When the moon is full, she has to boil her ring for five minutes and then she lights candles and sprinkles olive oil and chants, 'I am the wind,' or something, and then she has to wear the ring all the time after that, and if anybody steals it, something awful will happen." Mouse was quiet for a moment. "That book is giving me nightmares, and I'm only halfway through."

"Do you want me to read for a while?"

"I can't let anybody have it, Daddy says. It's a rare edition, and he even makes me wash my hands before I pick it up. It's awful, you know, what witches can do. The chapter I'm reading now says that if a witch is very skillful, she can murder a victim when he's just the right age for her coven and then bring him back to life at some time in the future when the hour is right."

Lynn turned her head slowly. "What's the right age?"

"It said, 'Young womanhood or manhood is the best

55

time for becoming an apprentice witch or warlock.' And it said that drowning is the preferred method of murder, because it 'preserves the body without blemish.' Honest Lynn, that's exactly what it said."

Lynn thought it over. "Well, Judith's certainly the right age, but I don't think Mrs. Tuggle is going to drown her for later. She must need her now. That's why she's been teaching her so much. In fact, Mrs. Tuggle might have her eye on half the girls in town!"

"I don't think so." Mouse adjusted her glasses and sat up straight. "The book says that only a gifted few are called upon to become witches or warlocks, and that a seventh-power witch sometimes has to wait years before she finds all the right people for her coven."

"I wonder how she picked Judith," Lynn mused. "I mean, do sparks fly or cats meow or something when the right person enters the room? Do you suppose Mrs. Tuggle gave Judith an aptitude test?"

"Maybe when they were sewing together they pricked their fingers and the blood matched," said Mouse. "Just think, a long time ago somebody must have discovered Mrs. Tuggle and turned her into a witch."

"And when Judith grows up, she'll find somebody else to teach," said Lynn. She was silent for a moment, and then, softly, she began to repeat the verse she had heard Judith chanting:

> *From the shadows of the pool,*
> *Black as midnight, thick as gruel,*

Come, my nymphs, and you shall be
Silent images of me.

"Good Lord!" shivered Mouse. "What's that?"

"Judith's chant," Lynn replied grimly.

At the bottom of the Morley steps, they stopped and went over the plan once more. They would wait until Judith left her room. Then Mouse would keep watch while Lynn went up and stole the doll from the blue box. They would bury it later.

Slowly they went up the walk and then on up the steps to the porch. There was no sound at all from inside—not even Stevie's monotonous little hum as he went about his play, or the *thunk* of his blocks on the bedroom floor. Lynn was uncomfortable when she left him alone in the house with Judith.

"Stevie?" Lynn called. There was no answer.

Suddenly Judith appeared from nowhere, standing in the doorway of the kitchen. Mouse gave a muffled squeak.

"Stevie's at a birthday party. He'll be home after a while, and I'm going down to the creek to swim. I don't want you following me. Do you understand?" Her voice sounded strange and far away.

Lynn didn't answer. She couldn't. Because there on Judith's hand was a ring that she had never seen before —a shiny silver ring, obviously new.

The back screen slammed and Judith's footsteps

sounded on the steps.

"Mouse, did you see it?" Lynn cried. "The ring!"

Mouse nodded. "And the way she looked at us!"

They raced to the dining room window. Judith was just leaving the garden and starting down the path through the high weeds. Finally only her dark hair was visible above the bushes, and then she was out of sight.

"She's gone," Lynn said. "You stay right here and watch. Yell if you see her coming back."

With her heart beating rapidly, Lynn hurried up the stairs. Slipping past the drawn curtain into the forbidden room, the enormity of what she was about to do made her jump at every creak or moan of the old beams. The room looked exactly as it had before, with the broom in one corner, and the purple candle on the bureau. The tip of the candle was black. It had definitely been used.

Lynn's eyes scanned the length of the dresser till they fell on the blue satin box, sitting amid a clutter of stuffed kittens and photo albums and hair curlers.

Lynn stretched out her hand, then paused. She was almost afraid of what she might find in it—something dead, perhaps, or shark's teeth or crow's feathers.

"Hurry up!" came Marjorie's whispered voice from the bottom of the stairs. "I get the creeps down here alone."

Swiftly Lynn picked up the box and opened it. The box was empty. Putting it back in place, she turned and rushed down the stairs.

"She *knows!*" she breathed, wide-eyed. "She knows we were coming to get the doll! It's gone!"

"I'll bet it's not far away," said Mouse, more determined than ever, "not when she can work such good spells with it. She's probably got it with her. If she's swimming, it'll be there on the bank. All you have to do is take it." Mouse was incredibly brave when it came to assigning jobs to other people.

"You heard what she said about following her." Lynn hesitated.

Mouse looked her straight in the eye. "If you had a stomachache like I had a stomachache," she said, "you wouldn't waste a single minute." And so it was settled.

They knew that Judith would be watching the house, so they went down the street to Lindon's Corner, hiked to the creek from there, and started back up again on the other side. There were blueberry bushes to hide them all the way, and it was the direction from which Judith would least expect them.

Carefully they made their way along, stopping every few feet to look up over the top of the bushes. They heard her voice before they came in sight of her—her bell-like laughter ringing out over the field, as though she were casting a spell on the grackles and crows that lived along the creek. Then they saw her kneeling on the bank at the water's edge, her long hair hanging down over the shiny ripples, arms outstretched. Suddenly she

jerked her head back so that the dark hair flew upward and cascaded down around her shoulders.

"Rise, oh creature of the depths!" she chanted.

Lynn and Marjorie strained to see as slowly two legs began to emerge from the surface of the water, feet first, till they stuck straight up in the air. Then there was a great splash, and a boy about Judith's age rose up out of the water, rubbing his face with one hand, looking foggily up at the sorceress on the bank who had conjured him up.

"Ah!" Judith cried, clapping her hands in delight. "It worked."

It was a boy Lynn and Mouse had never seen before in their lives. He had pale skin and pale hair, and moved slowly through the water toward Judith, shaking the water from his head.

At that moment Stevie's voice sounded faintly from across the meadow. "Lynn! Judith! I'm home."

Instantly Lynn began to back down the row of blueberry bushes, creeping silently so as not to attract attention, Mouse close behind her. They continued to move slowly, cautiously, until they reached the sycamore grove where they could finally stand up. A crow looked down at them beadily and gave a shrill caw.

There were too many strange things happening now to begin to understand them all. Lynn thought again of the tadpoles, the chant, and the strange boy there in the water.

"Who could he possibly have been?" Mouse said at last, when she'd stopped trembling. "Have you ever seen Judith with him before?"

"I've never seen Judith with *any* boy before," Lynn told her. "And that one certainly doesn't live around here."

"Well, the doll wasn't on the bank with her. I had a good look, and I didn't see it anywhere. That leaves only one place it could be. Mrs. Tuggle's. We'll have to think up an excuse to go there."

Lynn felt exhausted from the tension. "I've got to take care of Stevie till Mother gets home," she said. "Wait till 4:30, and then we'll go."

They sat on the porch and watched Stevie play with a paper airplane he had won at the party. As soon as Mrs. Morley got home and began making dinner, they started up the steep hill to the house at the top.

"I suppose she knows we're coming," Mouse said when at last they reached the steps. "She can sense it somehow."

"If she knows we're coming, then she knows what we're here for," Lynn said. "We've got to be very careful. Somehow we've got to think of an excuse to get up to her sewing room."

There was a brass knocker on the front door, which looked like a troll with its tongue hanging out. Lynn had never really looked at it closely before, but now, as she stared, the creature seemed to roll its eyes.

"Mouse!" she said quickly. "Did you see that?"

"What?" bleated Mouse, grabbing hold of her arm.

But the door was opening slowly to reveal a small woman in a blue print dress, and her eyes were even stranger than those of the troll.

As Mrs. Tuggle emerged from the shadows of the great hallway, Lynn saw that one of her eyes was gray and the other green, an oddity she had never noticed before on anyone else. Both eyes were small and seemed to peek out slyly from under her black bushy eyebrows.

"Well, now! Look who's come to pay me a call! The house isn't quite vitty, but come in anyway, and have some cake!"

62

"Oh, we can't eat anything!" Mouse said hurriedly. "We just had lunch. I mean, supper. I mean, it will be suppertime soon . . ."

"A little bit of cake won't hurt you," said Mrs. Tuggle, not to be put off. She led the way to the parlor and promptly disappeared into the kitchen.

"Now!" Mouse whispered, giving Lynn a shove. "Go look for the doll!"

"Already?" Lynn choked. "We just got here."

"You might not get another chance. Hurry! Go on! And for goodness' sake, don't eat anything she gives you!"

Lynn started toward the doorway on the opposite side of the room when suddenly she was confronted by Mrs. Tuggle, carrying a plate of cake.

"I—I just wanted to look at this photo on the table," Lynn stammered, changing direction. She moved over to a table in one corner and picked up an old picture of a young boy.

"One of my treasures," Mrs. Tuggle said. "But a sad thing it is."

"Why?"

" 'Twas my brother at six, when I was a young girl on the Isle of Man. That's where Castletown is, you know. I married, then, and my husband and I brought him with us when we came to America. My mother was dead, and he'd none to take him in but me. For ten years he lived here, and didn't I love him, though!"

She sat down on the old brown sofa and placed the cake on the table.

"I watched him grow, I did. Saw him start school and ride a bike, and before I knew it he was a fine young lad of sixteen. And then one day he was gone. Disappeared so sudden it was like the bogles themselves had carried him off, and nobody saw him for two days. Then, of a Friday, my husband went down to the creek —'twas more like a river, then—and he saw the body, floating face down, it was. We buried the poor lad down at the cemetery."

"Who killed him?" Mouse asked, and the directness of her question startled even Lynn.

The old woman's eyes narrowed, and she looked intently at Marjorie. "Why, nobody killed him, child! 'Twas an accident, but how, we'll never know."

The girls sat like statues, scarcely daring to breathe. The room seemed enormously large, and darker than it had been when they entered. And yet, it seemed strangely alive, as though even the figures on the wallpaper were watching.

"If ever you go across to the cemetery," the old woman continued, "take a bunch of posies for me and put it on his grave. You'll not have trouble finding it, for it's graced by two white angels holding a scroll between them."

Mouse, who was already sitting on the edge of her chair, slid halfway off and decorously scooted back up again. Slowly the girls exchanged a look of horror.

"Go on, have a piece of cake," Mrs. Tuggle urged, watching them.

"Oh, I just can't!" Lynn said. "But maybe I could take some home with me and save it till later."

"Of course. And if you're wanting more, I've plenty." The old woman sat quietly for a moment, then rambled on:

"Yes, it happened once in England, too, in the North Country, I heard. 'Twas a girl then, a wee one of three. She slipped out one night in the marsh, and a bad time it was, because the copse was all in bogs then, great pools of dark water, so they said, and creeping rivulets of green water and squishy mools, which sank if ever you stepped on them."

The hair on the back of Lynn's neck seemed to rise two inches.

"Some said it was the work of witches, so they sent out three men to seek her, and each of the three puts a stone in his mouth and a hazel twig in his hand, and he vows not to say a word till he's home safe again. Well, they went along and went along, and the moon lit up the bog pools. There were shadows here and shadows there, waving rushes and trembling mools, and great black trees all twisted and bent. And sudden they came upon a box, half hidden it was, like a coffin, with a cross, you know. And one of them up and forgets and speaks out loud, and says 'Our Lord,' first forward, because of the cross, and then backward, to keep off the bogles, and when the other two men heard what he'd spoke aloud, they up and ran home to get away from the quicks and the things that dwelt there, and the middlin' man, he sees what he's done, so he thinks, 'Well, I've done for it, now,' so he might as well open the coffin anyway. So he pulls and he tugs and pushes, and finally the lid tumbles off and there's naught but the little girl's fingers and toes. An' some say if he hadn't spoke aloud, 'twould have been the whole girl herself ready to come home."

Lynn knew that if they listened to any more, they would be in no condition to look for the doll.

"I guess we've got to be getting home," she said. "Do you mind if we use your bathroom, Mrs. Tuggle?"

"Do go," Mrs. Tuggle said, pointing to the stairs. "Turn left to the second door."

They started up the dark narrow stairs, clinging to each other as they went. From down below they could hear the old woman crooning one of the tunes that Judith sometimes hummed.

At the top of the stairs, they turned left, passed the first door, passed the bathroom, and tiptoed on to the sewing room. Softly Lynn turned the knob. The door creaked as it came open. There was the sewing machine, a pile of unhemmed skirts, a sewing basket and shears, and, on the end of the table, Judith's doll in the red plaid skirt, with pins sticking through the cloth and deep

into the doll's abdomen.

Grabbing the doll, Lynn stuffed it under her shirt and gently closed the door again behind them. They crept into the bathroom, flushed the toilet, and stepped back out into the hall.

Thunk, thunk, thunk. With wide eyes the girls stood motionless, ears attuned to each little sound. *Clump, clump, clump.* There were footsteps on the floor above them, crossing over their heads.

Bumping and pushing, the girls rushed back toward the stairs leading down, but the footsteps were already descending from above, and suddenly a door behind them opened and there stood the strange boy that Judith had conjured up out of Cowden's Creek.

Without a word, the girls clattered back down and, not even waiting to say good-bye to Mrs. Tuggle, raced out the front door, down the steps, and across the lawn.

"It's him!" Lynn panted. "It's Mrs. Tuggle's brother! She killed him, Mouse! I just know it! And Judith's brought him back. Oh, Mouse, what are we going to do?"

chapter five

The doll lay buried beneath a rose bush at the side of the house. Lynn had stuffed it in an empty oatmeal box, Mouse had dug the hole, and together they covered it with dirt so the blame would fall on each alike. There was nothing else to do now but wait for the next awful thing to reveal itself.

It was something of a hideous game, Lynn decided the next morning at breakfast. She felt sure that Judith and Mrs. Tuggle knew exactly what had happened to the doll, but could no more accuse Lynn of taking it than she could accuse them of sorcery. All were waiting till the time was right, and no one knew when that would be.

Whether Mother knew or suspected was another question. Sometimes Mrs. Morley seemed to be in another world. There were moments when she stared at Lynn for the longest time, and then, when Lynn asked why she was staring, Mother didn't even realize she had been. Or Lynn would go into the kitchen and ask a question, and instead of answering, Mrs. Morley would turn and say, with a look of utter fascination on her face, "I've just got the most wonderful idea for a book."

That was another thing about Mother. Every book she had ever written was conceived with the same great rush of inspiration, the growing excitement, the tumble of ideas that kept her scribbling constantly on little pads of paper she kept about the house, always sure she was on the brink of the best book yet.

But it never was, according to Mother herself.

"It's not the way I dreamed it," she always said when she sat down with the completed manuscript in her hand, exhausted from the work. "But it's the best I can do for now."

Sometimes she would say, "It's *almost* what I dreamed, but not quite." Or sometimes, "It's not at all what I had in mind." Like a composer searching for the perfect melody that was imprisoned somewhere in his own head, Mother was searching for the perfect story, always so sure at first that she had found it, and so resigned afterward to making do with second best.

She was at a moment of peak inspiration the day after

the doll was buried, however. Lynn found her making heaps and heaps of scrambled eggs before she realized that she was right there in the house on Locust Street, and there were already enough eggs for a regiment.

"Oh, Lynn, I've got the most wonderful idea for my book!" Mother said, staring at the eggs as though she'd never seen them before. "It's about . . . oh, no, I couldn't tell you . . . it would ruin it all . . . but I've got it all worked out in my head, and all the pieces fit together—all the loose ends I've been trying to sort, and I just can't wait to get going again. If I just had the time—the *time*—I could do it in three weeks. The words are just rolling in."

Mother never talked about a book she was working on until the first draft was finished. It wasn't mere superstition. She said she needed to keep that bubble of enthusiasm about her in order to finish it, and if anybody raised objections or pointed out flaws or frowned just a little, the bubble would burst. Better to keep it all to herself till the first sketch was down on paper, she always said. And then she couldn't stop talking about it. The day she completed a book, she told you about it whether you wanted to listen or not.

"Oh, you'll love it!" she would say to Judith or Lynn, whichever was handy. "It's about a boy who travels to Puerto Rico with his parents, but somehow he gets separated from them, and . . ."

"I don't like stories about boys," Lynn might say, but

71

it wouldn't stop Mother.

"You'll like this one," she would promise. "You like storms, don't you? And shipwrecks? And . . ."

The very worst thing Lynn could say to Mrs. Morley was that it sounded a lot like another book she had read. This seemingly innocent statement could throw her mother into near panic.

"*What* book? Who wrote it?" she would gasp, and go flying off to the library to locate a copy. If indeed it was similar to the book she had written, she would spend weeks rewriting her manuscript, muttering about the nuisance of ESP or whatever it was that put the same idea in two different authors' heads.

It was impossible to try to read one of Mother's books with her around. She would lean over the back of the chair each time she passed.

"Hmmmm, you're on chapter three," she would say. "Wait till you get to chapter five. That's where it gets funny." Or worse yet, she would seat herself across the room and if you so much as yawned while you read, or got up to stretch, she would say anxiously, "What's the matter? Don't you like it?"

And so, on this particular morning, Lynn found the house activated by Mother's newfound energy. Everything seemed to be moving at a faster pace. Dishes were whisked onto the table and off again, clothes were dumped in the washer and yanked out again. There were scribbled notes taped to the refrigerator and the cupboard doors, on top of the mantel, and next to the stairs. Mrs. Morley had every hour of her day allotted so that she wouldn't waste even a minute, and left for her studio early. It was no use trying to talk to her again about Judith. An idea was like a new baby, and once Mother got one, she couldn't put it down.

Lynn was lying lazily on her back on the floor of the music room when Mrs. Morley got home at four. The afternoon sun came through the stained glass insets of the bay window in just such a way as to cast a montage of reflections on the wall. Lynn liked to watch the changing patterns of sunlight; it gave her time to think.

As soon as they got up the nerve, she and Marjorie were going back to the cemetery to see if the angels with the scroll looked the least disturbed—they and the grave beneath them. And then there was this horrible wait to see what Judith and Mrs. Tuggle would do next, now that the boy had joined their coven. What was a male witch called—a warlock? Isn't that what Mouse had told her?

Mother looked at Lynn and immediately started to chuckle.

"Mrs. Tuggle told me about your visit yesterday," she said, kicking off her sandals. "She said that her grandson took you by surprise, and that you and Marjorie ran home so fast she couldn't even introduce you."

Lynn took her eyes off the reflections on the wall and

looked at her mother. "Her grandson? Is that what she told you?"

"Yes. I haven't met him yet, but she said he arrived a few weeks ago and will be here till the middle of August."

"So where's he been all this time?" Lynn quipped. "Chained in the basement?"

Mrs. Morley leaned against the doorway of the music room and stood looking down at her daughter. "Now what's that supposed to mean?"

Lynn sat up. "Mother, doesn't it seem strange that a boy would be staying at Mrs. Tuggle's for weeks and Judith would be going over there every other night and not say a single word about him? Don't you see anything odd in that at all?"

"Well, now that you mention it, I guess it does seem rather strange, except that Judith is fourteen, and when girls are that age, there are a lot of strange things you can't explain, particularly where boys are concerned."

"What else did Mrs. Tuggle tell you about him?"

Mrs. Morley shrugged. "Not much. She said he's shy, interested in astronomy, and is making some sort of chart of the stars from up there on the hill."

"Have you seen him, Mother?"

"No. Is he all that frightening?"

Lynn bit her lip. "Mother, have you ever heard of bodily transportation? I mean, a person sent to another place in time or made to disappear and show up somewhere else?"

Mrs. Morley slowly shook her head, and her eyes crinkled into a full smile this time. "Oh, Lynn, Lynn! You and your imagination! You remind me of myself when I was young. Now what have you decided about that boy? You're going to have him as scared of you as you are of him."

Lynn stretched out on the floor again. "Nothing," she said. "Skip it." The time would come when Mother would have to believe—when the facts would be so obvious she couldn't ignore them any longer.

"What shall I make for dinner, kids?" Mrs. Morley called from the kitchen. "Hamburgers or chili?"

"Hamburgers!" yelled Stevie, and at once the kitchen was filled with the clatter of dishes and Mother's quiet humming. That everything should seem so calm on the surface only made the caldron underneath more terrifying.

"Mouse," Lynn whispered that night when she phoned, "tell me exactly what that book said about selecting a witch or a warlock for a coven and drowning him and bringing him back to life later on. I need details."

"Just a minute," said Mouse, and returned with the book. "Chapter five, page 296:

Though authorities in the matter have argued among themselves, most agree that every man or woman possesses a certain potential for power through witch-craft, but only a very few will be chosen to become

75

expert in the art. A witch of the seventh power may look for a considerable length of time, even years, before selecting another to belong to her coven. Since the years of young maidenhood or manhood are the most successful for inducing a witch or warlock to join a coven, youth of such ages are greatly sought after by the witches on the continent of Europe. Some, in their search, have mastered the art of murdering their apprentices and restoring them to life at a later date when there is a greater number to form a coven. Drowning is the preferred method of murder because it preserves the body without blemish. A person so revived has no memory of his previous life and is solely in the power of the witch superior.

"Mrs. Tuggle told Mother he was her grandson," Lynn said. "Clever, isn't she?"

"She must be getting ready for something big," Mouse mused. "You just don't go around pulling a guy up feet first for nothing."

"Maybe she figures that with both her brother and Judith to help, she can raise the cone of power and do almost anything she wants," Lynn suggested. "Listen, Mouse, does the book tell how you can recognize a witch? Something that makes it sure?"

Mouse thumbed through the pages. "Well, it says they keep the ashes from their spells in a little black box, rub their bodies with parsley and belladonna, slack their thirst with salt, and are partial to the meat of babies and young children."

Again and again the same thought came back to her, and Lynn felt cold all over: Stevie.

Several weeks passed. Judith told her mother that her styling manikin was missing, but Mrs. Morley said she hadn't seen it. No one asked Lynn, and she said nothing. The doll was not mentioned again.

Majorie's parents had taken her to Ohio for five days, and she had smuggled the witchcraft book along with her. Lynn spent her time watching over Stevie, careful not to leave him alone for long with Judith. Twice more, when she was almost asleep, Lynn heard the tinkle of a bell from Judith's side of the curtain. The girls said less and less to each other.

It was obvious that Judith was seeing the boy she had conjured up. But she never talked about him. Instead of three or four times a week, Judith began going to Mrs. Tuggle's every evening. And sometimes, in the middle of the day, she announced that she would be gone for several hours. When Lynn asked where she would be, Judith replied, "Just walking." Lynn never saw where she went, and once, when she tried to follow, she found that Judith had simply vanished.

The Saturday that Marjorie came back, the girls met at the dairy store on Lindon's Corner and bought a two-dip. Slowly they walked out West Road, licking the pistachio off their cones, glad to be together again. But Marjorie was subdued. She had finished reading the book on witchcraft and seemed unusually sober.

"Lynn," she said, after a quick account of her Ohio cousins, whom she found very dull, "do you think it's possible for a person to get in trouble just by reading about witchcraft? I mean, if a person knows a lot of the secrets of sorcery and everything, and then doesn't use them, do you suppose something happens to her?"

Lynn shrugged. "I don't know. I study fractions at school but I never use them. Nothing ever happens to me. Why do you think it would?"

Marjorie's nose wrinkled a few times over her ice cream cone. "The last chapter said that if you summon the devil and then don't give him a task to do, he'll strangle you."

"So make sure you don't raise the devil," Lynn said, trying to be funny.

But Mouse didn't laugh. After they had walked a few more minutes in silence, she said, "Another thing they do is cavort in a nine-foot circle."

"What?" said Lynn. "Who?"

"Witches. They draw a circle on the floor with chalk and then cavort around in it. And they can't have any more witches in the coven than can cavort freely in a nine-foot circle."

"Do you suppose Mrs. Tuggle knows how to cavort?" Lynn said. For some reason the thought of the old

78

woman in a high-spirited dance made her laugh, but Mouse was anxious, not amused.

"Mouse, what's the matter?" Lynn asked finally. "Did you find out something in that book you're not telling me?" Her cone gone, Lynn wiped her hands on her jeans and faced Mouse.

Mouse thrust her hands in her pockets and went on trudging up the bank to the meadow along West Road. "Yeah," she said finally. "It—it doesn't sound so good, Lynn."

"What, Mouse? For heaven's sake, tell me!"

Marjorie took a deep breath. "It said that before a witch can attain her full power, she has to murder one of her younger brothers or sisters."

Lynn put her hands over her mouth and stared at Mouse in horror.

"Now I understand why Mrs. Tuggle killed her brother," Mouse went on. "And by drowning him, too, when he was just becoming a young man, she not only got her full power but set the stage for bringing him back later when she needed him for a coven."

Lynn couldn't move. Her eyes were huge. "Oh, Mouse! I just can't believe! . . . I just can't believe that Judith would drown anybody, especially Stevie!"

"She wouldn't have to," Mouse told her. "The book said that some witches manage to put their younger brother or sister out on the step at midnight on a night when there's a full moon, because that's when witches ride, and they'll swoop down and carry the child off. That's supposed to work just as well. I can see Judith putting Stevie out on the step, can't you? Or getting you outside at midnight?"

"Yes," Lynn said softly. "I guess I can. When—when is the next full moon, Mouse?"

"August 12. Next Saturday. I already checked."

"Then I'll sit up and keep watch," Lynn said determinedly. "Anybody tries to put Stevie out on the steps, I'll wake the whole neighborhood. Just let them try, and . . ."

The girls stopped in their tracks, because there in the tall grass was a human hand, and a moment later Judith's face appeared through the weeds. She was sitting there.

Instantly she scrambled to her feet and faced them, her voice low and strained. "Lynn Claire Morley," she hissed, as though intoning the name over a mixture of eucalyptus leaves, "I know what you're up to, even before you do it. This is the last warning. If you spy on me again, I'll make you so sorry, you'll wish we'd never been born sisters."

Lynn was sorry already. Without another glance at Judith, she fled across the open field, running as though Judith had unleashed the devil himself, Mouse at her heels.

They did not stop till they reached the south entrance of the cemetery, with its high iron gate that had long since rusted open and swung, creakily, on its upper hinge.

"Lynn!" Mouse panted. "She wasn't alone. I don't know who it was, but I saw some fingers there in the grass."

"Loose fingers?" Lynn bleated.

"I—I don't know. But they moved!"

"Oh, Mouse, I'm scared," Lynn said. "It gets worse all the time."

The tall trees stood like silent sentinels, sheltering the graves beneath. There was a haze in the air that seemed strange for August—warning of a storm, perhaps —of something about to happen.

"Mouse, do you feel it, too?" Lynn asked, looking cautiously around, still breathless from running.

"Yes, but I don't know what it is. Like—almost like someone else had just been here."

"I know. Creepy, isn't it?"

Lynn's heart beat faster as they approached the grave with the angels. The stones of Elfreda Lewis and her husband were in the same position they had always been, but still the feeling remained.

Slowly she turned toward the angels, and then she screamed. The two marble statues stood still and white as they always had, their lidless eyes looking out into nothingness, their long graceful fingers carved into the edge of the scroll, which they held between them. Tied tightly about the neck of one, however, was Judith's

yellow ribbon, as though someone had found it there in the grass and put it up where the loser might find it eventually. But there was something about the way it was tied, with a big knot at the angel's throat, that seemed far too deliberate somehow. And as Lynn stared in horror, the marble face seemed to smile at her menacingly for one brief moment before resuming its somber pose.

Up until that moment, Lynn hadn't really been sure. At first, she admitted, it had been partly a game that she and Mouse had enjoyed together. But no more. As the weeks had passed and one awful discovery had led to another, Lynn had decided it was a game no longer, nor was it a joke or a coincidence. The terror of what was happening replaced any excitement she had experienced before, and the one feeling that stayed in the pit of her stomach all day was fear. It would not go away. It was time, she decided on Monday, to talk to her father.

Mother was so wrapped up in her book that she simply did not know what was happening with Judith. She went to her studio in the mornings even before Lynn was up, and came home in the afternoon with the chapter she was writing so she could work on it later in the evening. Clothes were mended while she listened to the evening newscast. Meals were cooked in double amounts so that she could freeze a batch for the following week and save still more time. If anyone wanted to tell her something that took longer than thirty seconds, she would say cheerfully, "Come talk to me while I sort the clothes," or "Read it to me while I do the dishes." If she had been born with a third or fourth arm, Lynn was sure it would have been working steadily as well. And every so often, after Stevie had gone to bed, Mother would look up blankly from the big chair in the living room where she wrote when she was home and say, "*That's* the way I'll end that chapter," or, "I wonder how this paragraph should begin."

Mr. Morley was out in the street washing his car, and Stevie was there also, in his bathing trunks, holding the hose so that the water splashed all over the car and himself as well, his eyes tightly closed.

"Want to help?" Father said when he saw Lynn coming down the walk.

"No, thanks. I'll just sit and watch you slave," Lynn said, and perched on the bottom step. She couldn't talk with Stevie around.

Mr. Morley was wearing his oldest pants, a pair of basketball shoes he had inherited at college, and no shirt at all. He would have made a good father for Mouse, Lynn was thinking, and Mouse's father, who went to his bookstore each day in impeccable suit and tie, would have suited Judith and her immaculate taste to perfection.

"What's up?" Mr. Morley said, his long arm sweeping over the top of the car.

"Not much."

"Haven't tripped over that Beasley girl's bicycle recently. Did she ever get back from Ohio?"

"Yes. Last Saturday."

Stevie dropped the hose suddenly and his teeth were chattering. "I guess I've done enough," he said. "You can finish the rest if you want to."

"Hey, thanks, sport!" said his father. "You'd better go

get a shirt on. Your lips are blue."

Stevie went slowly up the steps sideways, putting both feet on each step to see the wet imprint they made. When he reached the walk at the top, he ran as fast as he could to the house and the screen door banged. Lynn went over to the car.

"Dad," she said, "do you believe that things sometimes happen that nobody can explain—scientists or anybody?"

"Sure. All the time."

She hesitated. This was too easy. She had thought Mom had believed too, when she hadn't.

"Have you ever heard of bodily transportation and witches raising up dead people to be in their covens or children being carried off at midnight when there's a full moon?"

"Yes, and I think it's a nice, fat bowl of malarkey," said Mr. Morley.

Lynn stared at him hopelessly. "But you said . . ."

"I said there are a lot of things we don't understand," Mr. Morley corrected. "Just because something happens and we don't understand it, doesn't mean that witches are responsible. Hand me that other rag, would you, Lynn? Now, that's a clean car if I ever saw one!"

After dinner the following Friday, Lynn found her mother packing a suitcase. She stopped at the door of her parents' room and stared. "Where are you going?"

"This is the writers' conference in Illinois that I told you about, honey. Dad and I are going to drive over there tomorrow morning and make a little holiday out of it. We'll be back Sunday evening."

Lynn stared. "You mean . . . Stevie and I will be here all alone with Judith?"

"During the day, but tomorrow night Mrs. Tuggle's coming down to stay with you."

"Mrs. Tuggle!" The words came from Lynn's throat with a shriek.

Mrs. Morley looked up. "Lynn, whatever is the matter with you?"

There was no time to lose. Lynn went on into the bedroom and shut the door behind her.

"Mother!" she said earnestly. "You *can't* leave us with Mrs. Tuggle! You don't know! Something awful is going on!"

This time Mother seemed annoyed. "What are you talking about?"

"Mother, I know you don't believe me, but Mrs. Tuggle is a witch. She's the one who's teaching Judith witchcraft. Judith has a candle in her room and a broom, and she does things with them. I know! And Mouse and I think that a long time ago Mrs. Tuggle drowned her brother in Cowden's Creek, and the boy at Mrs. Tuggle's isn't her grandson at all, but the boy who was drowned, bodily transported, because we saw Judith conjure him up out of the creek, and—"

"Lynn!" Mother's voice was stern. "Now this is going just a little too far to be funny!"

"It's *not* funny, Mother! It's true, and I'm scared!"

"Now look, sweetheart. Mrs. Tuggle has been in this neighborhood a long time, and I haven't heard one thing to make me distrust her. You and Mouse are obviously taken with witchcraft these days, and your imaginations are working overtime. Dad and I have been looking forward to getting away for a day or two, and I don't think this is the time to bring up all this. You'll be perfectly safe with Mrs. Tuggle, and if there's any trouble, I'm sure the neighbors would help."

"But nobody knows she's a witch, Mother! No one would believe me!"

"You're absolutely right, because Mrs. Tuggle is a dear, sweet woman who doesn't deserve to have her reputation ruined by two little gossips. Now I want you to do your best to get along with her. You might even enjoy it."

Lynn's legs felt weak, and tears came to her eyes.

"Mother!" she said desperately. "You *can't* leave me home with Judith! You just *can't*!"

"Now look, darling," Mrs. Morley said. "If you and Judith are having problems getting along together, you'll just have to work them out as best you can, that's all. Really, Lynn, you'll be okay. I just know it. You're getting yourself worked up over nothing."

Blindly Lynn started downstairs, and Mother called

after her, "Oh, Lynn, you are so much like I was at your age. The stories I could tell! Some day I'll have to sit down and tell you some of them."

Lynn did, however, succeed in making her mother uneasy.

"It's not that I believe any of her tales, it's just that I hate to leave the girls together when they're not getting along," Lynn heard her mother say to her father later.

"Mrs. Tuggle will be here to knock a few heads together if they get out of line," said Mr. Morley. "She'll manage."

There was silence for a moment. Then Mother said, "You know, we really don't know her very well, do we?"

"Who? Lynn?"

"Mrs. Tuggle. I mean, we've lived in this neighborhood all these years, but—well, we've never had her to dinner or anything. Maybe I don't know her as well as I thought."

"You've never heard anything bad about her, have you?"

"No . . . I really haven't heard much at all, one way or another."

"Come on, now. She's lived here longer than anybody else. The Edmunds left their children with her when they went to Europe last year, didn't they? Why don't you talk to them?"

"I can't," Mother fretted. "They moved away a few months ago. I wonder why. Does anybody know?"

"Look, Sylvia, you've got to live a little! As soon as you see a nice weekend coming, you get the worries."

Mother laughed nervously. "Bring on the joy!" she said. "I won't think about it again."

She did, though. Later, as Lynn was helping her mother put the laundry away, Judith passed them in the hall and brushed against Mrs. Morley.

"Ouch!" said Mother, rubbing her arm. "Good grief, Judith! You scratched me!"

"Sorry," Judith mumbled, and went on up the stairs to the third floor. Lynn stared at the marks on her mother's arm. Mrs. Morley was examining them, too.

"Those are the same kind of scratches she made on Stevie's arm, Mother, and on mine!" Lynn said.

Mrs. Morley pressed her lips together firmly and lifted the stack of towels to the top shelf of the linen closet. "All it means is that Judith hasn't been cutting her nails," she said tersely. "Now I'm *not* going to say another word about this, Lynn. I *refuse* to get involved in this nonsense."

Lynn went down to the living room and sat on the couch beside her father. She felt afraid and very much alone.

"Why the long puss?" he asked, turning the pages of the paper.

"I don't think Mom should be going," Lynn said in a voice barely audible. "I think she should stay home where she belongs and take care of us."

"Your mother belongs in a lot of different places, and home is only one of them. You children are old enough now to take over some of the responsibility yourselves, and this gives her a chance to do some of the other things she likes."

"She'd be sorry if anything happened to us," Lynn muttered.

"What could happen with Mrs. Tuggle here?" Father said, giving her a playful tap with his newspaper. "Come on, old girl, buck up. Even Stevie's taking it better than you."

Yeah, if Stevie only knew, Lynn thought. And suddenly she remembered. Stevie! Saturday night! The night of the full moon . . .

chapter six

Lynn could see it all clearly now—how perfectly it had all been arranged, how expertly the details had been planned. The Morleys would be gone, and Mrs. Tuggle would be in charge.

She had been awake for a half hour the following morning, wondering what to do, and was about to get up and call Mouse when she heard footsteps on the stairs. She lay very still, pretending sleep.

It was Mrs. Morley. Glancing over at Lynn, she softly pushed open the curtain to Judith's room and went in. Lynn waited, her ears straining to hear.

"Judith!" came Mother's voice. "Judith, wake up. It's almost time for us to leave, and I want to talk to you before I go."

"What about?" came Judith's sleepy reply.

"Are you awake?"

"I guess so. What's the matter?"

"I want to know something." The bed creaked as Judith turned over.

"What?"

"I want to know what this is."

There was silence.

"What is it? I can't see. . . ."

"It's a small black box filled with ashes, that's what."

"Give me that!" Judith's voice suddenly came alive. "You're not supposed to touch that."

"Why? What on earth? . . ."

"It's something of mine that's private, that's all. I wish you people would stay out of my things."

"I didn't get into your things," came Mrs. Morley's voice, still surprised. "I found it under the glider on the porch. I'm curious. What are they the ashes of?"

"Just—just something I want to keep, that's all."

Again there was a period of silence.

"Then why did you burn it?"

"I just wanted to."

"Where did you get this black box?"

"Mrs. Tuggle gave it to me."

"Judith." Mrs. Morley's voice was impatient. "Is there anything I should know before I go away this weekend? Anything at all?"

"What about?"

"About you . . . or Mrs. Tuggle?"

At that moment the third floor bedroom was enveloped in shadow, and a sudden rush of wind swept across the floor, billowing the curtain that separated the girls' rooms. There was a crash from Judith's side as a picture blew off the dresser.

"Ye gods, I'd better close the window!" said Judith, springing up. "It's going to blow my stuff all over."

"The wind started last night and has been unusually gusty," Mother said. "I'd better see about Lynn's windows." She stopped. "What about it, Judith? Is there anything I should know?"

"Of course not," said Judith. "Don't be silly."

Mother left, and Judith went back to bed. Lynn waited a little longer, her heart pounding, and then got up and went downstairs. A few minutes later Mother came through the hall with her suitcase and picked up Stevie. She held him very close for a moment and then gave him a big smacking kiss on the neck. "I'm going to miss my boy," she said. "You be a big help to Mrs. Tuggle, now, and show her where I keep things."

Mrs. Morley also hugged Lynn. "Now listen," she said, in a kind of forced cheerfulness. "Should anything happen and you need me, I left the phone number of the writers' conference by the telephone. But I'm sure everything is going to be fine. I have two lovely daughters I can trust, and I know you'll get along."

And then, as though she was afraid she would change her mind, she picked up her suitcase and followed Father down the walk.

"It's the old imagination working overtime!" Lynn heard her father saying jovially. "Probably a love letter Judith's burned and can't bear to throw away. You're just as bad as Lynn, honey! Worse, even! That's where the girl gets it—from you."

Lynn watched with sinking heart as the car pulled away with her parents in it. She felt helpless about the coming night.

"Mouse," she said over the phone, "it's awful! They're gone!"

"What? Who?"

"My folks. Mom is speaking at a writers' conference in Illinois and Dad drove her. They won't be back till tomorrow night."

There was silence from the other end. Then Mouse's voice came like a rush of wind over the wire. "Lynn! Tonight! The full moon! Didn't you tell them?"

"They didn't believe me," Lynn said miserably. "I tried. Oh, Mouse, what will I do? I'm scared. Can't you come over?"

"I've got a piano recital this afternoon," Mouse wailed. "I've got to play the Chopin 'Polonaise.'"

"You didn't tell me you were in a recital."

"That's because it's going to be awful. I hope nobody comes."

"Well, this is going to be awful, too."

"Listen, Lynn, whatever you do, don't eat any of Mrs. Tuggle's cooking. That's important. I know all about the potions they put in food. You'll fall asleep and won't wake up till tomorrow afternoon."

Lynn took a deep breath and tried to stop the panic.

"And Lynn—one thing more. Chapter thirteen, second paragraph: 'Dipping into milk or water is necessary before one can be transformed.' For goodness' sake, don't let Mrs. Tuggle give Stevie a bath."

Stevie came back in from the porch. He had dressed himself that morning and had his shirt on backward. Lynn helped him put it on again and tenderly combed his hair. How could Judith even consider getting rid of him, the chubby little child who called sandwiches "samwiches," and wanted to know if God ever wore boots? The house wouldn't be the same without Stevie. In fact, no matter what happened now, it would probably never be the same again. She silently made his breakfast.

"I like Mrs. Tuggle," Stevie said from the table, where he swung his legs back and forth and munched a piece of toast. "This is going to be fun, isn't it, Lynn?"

It was impossible to say yes.

"Why do you like Mrs. Tuggle so much?"

"Mommy left me with her once when she went shopping. And Mrs. Tuggle gave me candy and told me stories," Stevie said.

"What kind of stories did she tell you?"

Stevie thought about it, licking the jelly off the sides of his mouth. "About the hobyahs."

"The what?"

"The hobyahs. They burn down houses and kill the old man and woman and carry the little girl off in a sack."

Lynn said no more. Had Mother no sense? Didn't she see through Mrs. Tuggle at all? What would she say if she got back from Illinois and Stevie was gone?

Lynn sent him out to play in the sand and cleared off the breakfast dishes.

Judith came downstairs at eleven. She was wearing her best pair of jeans and a fresh polka-dot shirt. There was a touch of makeup on her face and small earrings in her pierced ears. This time her hair had been pulled back with a red scarf.

"Going somewhere?" Lynn asked, wondering.

"No. I'm just getting ready for the Tuggles. I think we should all look decent and straighten the house up a little if they're going to sleep here."

"What do you mean, 'they'?"

Judith seemed to avoid looking at her. "Mrs. Tuggle and her grandson, Clyde."

"He's sleeping here, too?"

"Why not? He can't very well stay in her big house alone if Mrs. Tuggle is going to be down here. He'll sleep on the back porch or somewhere."

Now it was three against two—Lynn and Stevie against two witches and a warlock.

"What's he like?" Lynn quizzed, trying to keep Judith talking.

Judith shrugged. "Nice. I hope you'll act civil while he's here, and that you and Marjorie won't go around hiding behind doors and acting like creeps."

She made it sound so natural, so normal.

"Have you seen my yellow ribbon?" she asked suddenly.

"W—what yellow ribbon?" Lynn stammered.

"The one I've been wearing all week," Judith said. "Have you seen it?"

The question was so direct that it took Lynn by surprise. "Why do you need it?" she asked in return. "You're wearing a scarf."

"It's important to me, that's why," Judith snapped. "Have you *seen* it?"

"I haven't seen it anywhere around the house," Lynn hedged.

Judith started through the hall to the living room and then turned around, one eyebrow raised. "Have you seen it *outside* the house, then?"

Lynn couldn't think of an answer.

"Lynn, I *mean* it!" Judith warned. "If you've seen my ribbon, tell me."

Lynn's mind raced. Judith didn't ask where it was; she knew. She wanted to know if *Lynn* knew. That was

97

the important thing. Maybe Lynn could bargain with her.

"Maybe I have, and maybe I haven't," Lynn answered. "If you talk Mrs. Tuggle out of coming here tonight, I'll tell you."

"Talk her out of coming! Why?"

There were footsteps on the back porch, and then Stevie's excited voice. "Hey, Judith! Look what I found!"

Both girls wheeled around, and there stood Stevie, his legs covered with dirt, holding a sand shovel in one hand and Judith's doll in the other.

"My manikin!" Judith cried. "Where did you find it, Stevie?"

"I was just diggin' around the rose bush and my shovel hit somethin' and I dug it up. It was an oatmeal box and I found the doll inside!" He beamed importantly.

Judith turned and stared at Lynn, the color rising in her face, but Lynn was not prepared for what happened next. Judith lunged at her, pinning her hard against the wall, her fingernails digging into Lynn's cheek.

"You took it! I know you did!" Judith shrieked, and she looked strangely flushed. Even her hands felt hot. "I've just had enough! You're always into my things! You always ruin my plans! Don't you ever take anything that belongs to me again! Ever! Ever! Ever!"

Lynn screamed, and Stevie started to cry. Judith

dropped her hands and stood there breathing hard.

"Do you know where that ribbon is?" she said through clenched teeth.

"Yes," Lynn replied weakly. "In the cemetery, on the angels . . ."

"You saw it then." Judith stared at her strangely for almost a full minute. Then she turned and walked quickly out the front door.

Lynn ran one hand over the scratches on her cheek, her heart pounding. She looked in the hall mirror and gasped, for the scratches were in the form of an X, as though she were marked for some dark purpose.

Stevie was whimpering. "You scare me when you fight," he said.

Lynn took him into the living room. She put Judith's doll on the mantel and then sat Stevie on her lap. It had been years since she and Judith actually had hit each other. She felt frightened at the intensity of Judith's anger, as though in her bewitchment Judith was just as helpless against Mrs. Tuggle's power as Lynn. It was as if the real Judith had disappeared and someone else were inhabiting her body. Lynn shivered.

"Listen, Stevie," she said quickly. "Judith isn't—she isn't feeling too good these days, I guess, and she might do some awfully strange things. I want you to listen carefully. Don't go anywhere at all with Judith. Do you understand me? You stay right where I can see you all the time, and tell me if she does anything that seems odd."

Stevie looked at Lynn anxiously. "I'll tell Mrs. Tuggle on her if she does."

"No, Stevie! Tell me! Mrs. Tuggle might do strange things, too. Just trust me. Nobody else. Okay?"

Stevie put his head against Lynn's shoulder. "I wish Mommy was home."

"So do I, Stevie. So do I."

When Judith came back later, she had the boy with her.

He was an inch shorter than Judith, with muscular

legs and arms and blondish hair that came down over his ears and curled down the back of his neck. His eyes were pale blue, and there was a starry look about his face, as though he had been born in another age and lived in a different time. He carried an astronomy book and a folder of papers and charts.

Lynn stared at him intently as he came in the house. Yes, no doubt about it, he looked like the picture of the drowned boy in Mrs. Tuggle's living room. Not exactly like it, of course, for the boy in the picture was only six, and he wasn't murdered till he was sixteen. But still the resemblance was striking.

"Lynn, this is Clyde Tuggle," Judith said with cold politeness. For a moment her eyes met Lynn's and there was a flicker of concern for the marks on her sister's cheek. Then her eyes seemed to turn into limpid dark pools of nothingness.

"Hi," said the boy.

"Hi," Lynn said back, unsmiling.

"Mrs. Tuggle will be down later," Judith said. She led Clyde out on the back porch. They sat down on the glider. The boy from Cowden's Creek opened his folder, took out a map of the heavens, and spread it across their laps.

Lynn listened to their whispered conversation, trying to find out what they had in mind. In every way possible, she had to ruin their plans for the evening. If necessary, she could even get Mouse to come over and spend the night. That way, the cone of power would have to work in several directions all at once, and maybe it wouldn't be strong enough to get Stevie outside at midnight.

About 4:30, Lynn was in the living room working on a puzzle with Stevie when the patch of sunlight on the floor faded away, the room grew darker, and a faraway rumble of thunder sounded from the north end of Cowden's Creek. Lynn looked around. Mrs. Tuggle was standing in the doorway, and Lynn jumped as though she had never seen the woman before in her life.

"Wasn't meaning to startle you," Mrs. Tuggle said quickly. "I've brought something from home for our supper, so I'll slide it into the oven." She went into the kitchen and opened the oven door.

Just like the witch in Hansel and Gretel, Lynn thought.

Shortly afterward the old woman came back into the living room. She was wearing an apron over her brown dress, and she sat down on a chair with her bony hands on her knees.

"Well! Well! Well!" she said, looking about her. "The house is all vitty, the children quiet, the kettle on for tea, and I'll not have much to do, will I?"

Did she only imagine it, Lynn wondered, or was there something malicious about Mrs. Tuggle's smile?

"Lynn's gonna take care of me while my Mommy's

away," Stevie told her.

"And a good sister she is, too!" Mrs. Tuggle said.

Thunder sounded again from the north and seemed to linger, rumbling along Cowden's Creek from one end of the town to the other.

Judith and the boy came in from the back porch.

"I think we'll take a walk before dinner, Mrs. Tuggle," Judith said. "Want me to set the table before we leave?"

"Best to go and get yourselves back before it storms," the old lady said. "Lynn and I will do for ourselves."

The screen door slammed behind Judith and Clyde. Mrs. Tuggle opened the lid of her sewing basket and took out a sleeve she was working on. Even that looked strange in her hands—an armless sleeve, attached to nothing. Out in the kitchen the kettle began to whistle softly, and the old woman let it sing.

There wasn't anything about Mrs. Tuggle that looked natural, Lynn decided. Her one gray eye and one green eye were somehow placed too close to the center of her face, crowding her long thin nose, which looked pinched in the middle. Her dark stockings were wrinkled about the ankles, and her fingers worked with the nimbleness of a woman who had done nothing all her life but sit in an attic and spin.

Stevie soon tired of the puzzle and forgot whatever feelings he was supposed to have against Mrs. Tuggle. He sauntered over and leaned on her chair, watching her needle speed in and out.

"Are you a brownie?" he asked finally, curious about her dark dress.

Mrs. Tuggle laughed, and one of her teeth flashed gold when her mouth opened. "Goodness no, child. A brownie is a sort of a bogle, you know, with pointy ears and hair all over."

"Is it bad?" Stevie wanted to know.

"Well, now, that's depending on how you look at it. If you have a treasure, you know, and you bury it, and you scatter drops of lamb's blood over it, a brownie will watch over it for you and frighten everyone else away. That's not so bad now, is it?"

Stevie thought it over. "Who kills the lamb?"

For a moment Mrs. Tuggle was taken aback. "Well, now, that I don't know, lad."

The house was quiet and the clock in the hall seemed louder than ever. Out in the kitchen the strange kettle continued its croon. Again the thunder and then the strange stillness, as though everything were waiting . . . waiting. . . .

"What if it's not a treasure that's buried?" Stevie went on, imagining. "What if it's a dead man? Will the brownie watch over him, too?"

That a boy, Stevie, Lynn thought. *Keep her talking.*

"Well now, lad, if it's a man that's died a natural death, he needs no looking after, you know, save by

God. And if it's a murdered man, well, then his bones might tell who did it."

"What do you mean, Mrs. Tuggle?" asked Lynn.

"They say that if a body's been murdered, his bones will speak out to anybody walking overhead, and say who 'twas that killed him. It's all a story, you know."

"What if it's not, though?" Lynn persisted, her thoughts speeding on ahead of her, wildly putting things together. "What if there was someone right here in our own cemetery who had been murdered, and the murderess wanted to stop his bones from talking?"

Mrs. Tuggle looked at Lynn, her needle pausing for a moment. "What a storyteller you are, child!" she said. "You'll be scaring your brother so he can't sleep."

Lynn ignored it. "Do you think the murderess would try to conjure him up again and turn him into a warlock or something?"

"Goodness, how you go on! That may be, but 'twould have to be witchcraft, for sure."

"How many witches do you think it would take, Mrs. Tuggle?" Lynn asked, her eyes looking straight into the old woman's face. "Would two be enough? One little one and one big one?"

Mrs. Tuggle didn't answer for a moment. She picked up the sleeve and began picking at it again. "That I don't know about, dear," she said, "and it's best we talk of something else with Stevie about, don't you think?"

Lynn said nothing more. Determined to stand her ground, however, she continued to stare in the old woman's face till Mrs. Tuggle noticed and looked up. For a full ten seconds they looked into each other's eyes, neither giving an inch. Then slowly Mrs. Tuggle's lips spread into a knowing grin, and the gold tooth shone brightly inside the dark cavern of her mouth.

chapter seven

The storm that had begun in the north was approaching steadily. Like a drummer leading the way, the thunder beat a quick cadence, paused, and beat another, growing louder with each one.

Lynn had taken a box of crackers and a jar of peanut butter to her room, and was just stuffing them under her pillow for her dinner later when she heard footsteps on the stairs, and the short figure of Mrs. Tuggle in her brown dress appeared in the doorway.

"It's supper waiting," she said. "I've been calling. . . ."

"I didn't hear you," Lynn said, and followed her down to the kitchen.

"It's the thunder, then. We're sure of a storm."

Supper was a strange affair. The boy from Cowden's Creek ate slowly, shyly, with his eyes on his plate. He broke his biscuit into pieces before he ate it, and then took one at a time, between bites of stew, as though performing a certain ritual.

Judith, too, was strangely distant. She even looked different, somehow—as though something physical were happening to her. When she talked at all, it was to Mrs. Tuggle, and then she sounded far more grown up than she was.

"I suppose we ought to give Stevie a bath and wash his hair," she was saying. "He was digging in the dirt this afternoon."

"I'll take care of that," Lynn said quickly.

"That's a good girl," said Mrs. Tuggle. "I'll tidy up the kitchen, and we'll have ourselves an evening to read and sew or whatever. Lynn, dear, eat of your stew before it cools."

Lynn picked up a forkful of meat and was so intent on bringing it to her mouth and dropping it discreetly into her hand that she almost missed what was happening to Stevie. Then it was too late.

The little boy had picked up another biscuit and was about to put it in his mouth when Mrs. Tuggle reached forward, grasped his hand in her own, and thrust his fingers into a cup of milk.

"Try that," she said, winking at Judith. "Nothing's so good as bread and cream, and if there's no cream to be had, milk is aplenty."

The biscuit was delivered to Stevie's mouth, and he ate it appreciatively, milk dripping from his fingers. Lynn stared. *Dipping into water or milk is necessary before one can be transformed,* Mouse had said. Mrs. Tuggle had done it, and Stevie was being prepared for his transformation. It did not really matter whether the witches planned to carry him off so they could eat of his flesh or boil him down for his fat. The damage had been done, and all Mrs. Tuggle need do now was wait until midnight.

Lynn remembered the story Mrs. Tuggle had told her about the men who went out to search for the little girl, and when they lifted the lid of the coffin, all they found were her fingers. Maybe that's all there would be left in Stevie's bed come morning.

Slowly Lynn looked about the table, a chill creeping over her, mingling with panic. The boy from Cowden's Creek continued his silent eating. Judith ate daintily, slowly. Every so often her eyes stole over to Clyde's and his to hers, and they exchanged a sort of smile. And across the table, the old woman in her brown dress watched Stevie with narrowed glinting eyes, smiling to herself and nodding strangely.

Suddenly there was a flash of lightning and an instant clap of thunder—a pause—and then a rush of rain, soft at first, then becoming louder and louder, hitting at the windows with a *rat-a-tat* sound. Mrs. Tuggle leaped up.

"Best to close all the windows till the storm goes by," she said.

"I'll get the uppers," said Clyde, suddenly coming alive, while Judith dashed into the living room. In that moment Lynn hurriedly scraped all the stew out of her bowl and dropped it in the garbage pail. On the counter she noticed some spices that the old woman had brought along—rosemary, sage, and parsley.

It was a storm such as Lynn had never seen before in Indiana. It came with such force that the rain fell sideways, in long streaks, and the wind shrieked shrilly around the windows and doors, like a concert of howling witches.

Upstairs, Judith and the boy from Cowden's Creek were clattering around closing windows, and Stevie raced after them yelping excitedly.

"Stevie, will you stop it?" came Judith's irritated voice from the stairs. "Whenever there's confusion, you have to make it worse."

Stevie came down ahead of them, leaning against the wall as he walked, lower lip sticking out.

"Honestly!" Judith sniped again when they reached the bottom. "You're enough to drive people wild."

There was a flash of lightning that illuminated the living room, as if a giant searchlight had flashed for a moment. The thunder was immediate, and the walls shook and trembled with the boom. Then the lights went out. Stevie shrieked and dived for Lynn, who stood in the middle of the rug. She put her arms around him, feeling his heart beating against her.

"I'll get some candles," Judith said, starting back upstairs again. "I've got some in my room."

"I'll go with you," said Clyde, and they disappeared into the darkness.

"It's upon us now," Mrs. Tuggle said, feeling her way across the room to a chair. Her hand brushed Lynn's cheek as she passed, and it was cold and dry, like a withered bone.

Lynn knelt down on the rug and pulled Stevie down beside her, afraid to be separated from him. Any moment something could happen—here in the house with darkness all around. She began to shiver involuntarily, an uncontrollable shaking that rattled her teeth. The panic that had begun when her parents left that morning was growing stronger. Over in the corner, Mrs. Tuggle began to mumble, as though speaking to someone who wasn't there.

There was a glow of light in the hallway, and Judith came in with a purple candle in her hands.

"And now we have light," Mrs. Tuggle said cheerily. "Oh, look at the poor things. Scared, are you?" she asked, bending toward Stevie and Lynn. "Why, I've seen worse in my time. Indeed I have." She settled back in her chair as Judith put the candle on the table beside her. " 'Twas in Castletown—I was but a girl, and

the night howled at my window with a gale off the Hebrides. I did not think I would ever see the morning light, so fierce it blew, as though the demons themselves were shrieking outside to carry me off. I will remember that storm to my grave, for I always believed it took a part of me with it."

Judith moved on about the room restlessly, from window to window, her shadow twisting and touching, dancing and darting, like some ghoul of the forest performing a ritual dance.

The clock in the hall chimed out eight o'clock. The side door rattled furiously in the wind as though spirits, beckoned by the purple candle, were trying to batter their way in. Another dart of lightning illuminated the room. Thunder followed, and the walls shook. More lightning, in rapid succession, and suddenly Judith's doll, which Lynn had propped up on the mantel, moved forward and fell on the brick hearth, its two legs broken.

Then, from Judith's throat, came a low sound—not a moan, not a sigh, but a strange kind of call, like that of an animal, and suddenly she began to recite the verse that Lynn had heard before:

> *From the shadows of the pool,*
> *Black as midnight, thick as gruel,*
> *Come, my nymphs, and you shall be*
> *Silent images of me.*

"Ah!" said Mrs. Tuggle. "Yes."

> *Suck the honey from my lips,*
> *Dance upon my fingertips.*
> *When the darkness tolls the hour,*
> *I shall have you in my power.*

And then in unison, their voices chanting:

> *Fast upon us, spirits all,*
> *Listen for our whispered call.*
> *Whistling kettle, tinkling bell,*
> *Weave your web and spin your spell.*

Slowly Lynn stood up, clutching Stevie to her, and began moving backward toward the telephone in the hallway, never taking her eyes off the shadowy figures before her.

Mrs. Tuggle clapped her hands suddenly. "Aye, that's enough of the dark poems. Stevie will lie abed all night with his eyes open. Let's have us some nursery rhymes, eh, to wait out the storm." And then, clapping her hands in time to her words, she began:

> *Bat, bat, come under my hat,*
> *And I'll give you a slice of bacon;*
> *And when I bake,*
> *I'll give you a cake,*
> *If I am not mistaken.*

"Come, Stevie. Come to Mrs. Tuggle, dear, and I'll tell you another:

Here comes a candle to light you to bed,
And here comes a chopper to chop off your head.

"Don't like that one, eh?"

Holding Stevie tightly by the hand, Lynn edged around the corner of the living room and into the hallway. Quickly she searched for the pad by the telephone on which Mother had written her number. The pad was blank. There was no writing on it at all.

Panic seized her as she entered the living room again.

"Where is that number Mother left by the phone?" she demanded, her voice shaking.

No one answered.

"Where is that number?" Lynn screamed. "She left it there for me."

"Lynn, dear, I'm sure it's around someplace. Best to wait till the lights come on again and then we'll all look for it," Mrs. Tuggle said. "Maybe the wind blew it about."

She was trapped. The trembling began again. Lynn wished desperately that Marjorie were there. What would she do when the awful moment came, and Stevie was being dragged outside on the steps? Run out in the street screaming? Call the police? Attack Judith? What chance did she have against the three of them? In the light of the candle, she could see Mrs. Tuggle sitting in the big chair next to the sofa, one hand on Judith's arm. And Judith, sitting next to Clyde, had one hand in his. An intimate coven of witches. Weren't they supposed to be touching to raise the cone of power? Wasn't that something Mouse had read?

And then, almost as suddenly as the storm had begun, it ceased. As Lynn listened to the sound of thunder in the distance, like some retreating army, she realized that the rain had quit and the wind had stopped its shrieking. There was no sound at all now from the outside but the dim roll of thunder to the south of Cowden's Creek, and the dripping of rain from the eaves.

As Mrs. Tuggle lit more candles and placed them around the rooms, she seemed like a harmless old lady going about her work, and Lynn felt suddenly tired from the tension.

"I'm going to give Stevie a bath and get him to bed," she said, picking up one of the candles.

"Have a good night, lad," Mrs. Tuggle said to Stevie. "It's good the wind is quitting now."

Slowly Lynn ascended the stairs to the second floor, the shadows edging along beside her, her legs weak. She set the candle on the sink and ran hot water into the tub, hoping Stevie would not notice how her hands were shaking.

"When will the lights come on, Lynn?" Stevie asked, as Lynn rubbed shampoo into his hair.

"Pretty soon, I imagine. We'll probably all go to bed early. Things will be okay in the morning." She knew it was a lie.

When Stevie was in his pajamas, Lynn picked up the candle again and tucked him in bed. Then she crouched down on the floor beside him.

"Listen, Stevie. If anybody comes in your room during the night, you call me, as loud as you can. I'll be awake."

"How will I know they come in if I'm asleep?" he asked.

"They might try to pick you up or wake you or take you somewhere. If anybody does, you call."

Downstairs, Mrs. Tuggle met Lynn in the hall.

"I just called the power company," she said. "The lights won't be on till morning. The shame it is. I guess I'll be doing dishes by candlelight. It's been many a year since I've done that. What a story we'll have for Mrs. Morley, eh? At least the phone is working." She went on past Lynn with her lighted candle and the small flame of light made her shadow even more grotesque.

The phone rang, and Lynn answered.

"Lynn?" came Mouse's voice. "Are you still there?"

"Barely."

"Can you talk? Is anyone listening?"

"I don't know. I'm not sure."

"Listen, do you want me to come over and stay all night?"

"Yes! Oh, please! Please!"

Suddenly Judith faced her in the hall.

"Marjorie can't stay over," Judith said. "Mother said

we weren't to have any girls in while she was gone."

"I heard that," Mouse said, after Judith had gone back in the living room.

"Oh, Mouse, what will I do?" Lynn said, tears filling her eyes.

"Lynn, listen. You sound scared to death. Just answer yes or no. Did you eat any of Mrs. Tuggle's food?"

"No."

"Did she give Stevie a bath or wash him up?"

"No, but . . ."

"But what? Did she dip him in water at all?"

"No . . ."

"In milk?"

"Yes."

"She dipped him in *milk*?"

"Just his fingers."

"That's probably all it takes. Lynn, I wish you could talk. Can't you tell me anything else?"

"Judith's sitting right around the corner," Lynn whispered.

"Do you think something's going to happen?"

"I'm sure of it."

"To Stevie?"

"Yes."

"Oh, Lynn! Is there anything I can do? Call the police?"

"What could we say? Who would believe us? Listen, Mouse, are your lights on yet?"

There was silence for a moment. Then the chills raced through her again as she heard Marjorie say, "Why, sure! They were never out."

By the time the storm had passed, night had gathered and the sky stayed dark. Stevie was soon fast asleep in his bedroom on the second floor. Lynn had considered putting him in her own bed, but then they would all ask why. If she kept her door open, however, she could look down the stairs into the hall below and see part of Stevie's doorway. She would stay up all night and keep an ear out for footsteps below.

Just as Mrs. Tuggle said they would, the lights stayed off. The old woman clattered about the kitchen, trying to get the dishes done, and Judith and Clyde sat on the sofa with a purple candle, examining a large chart of the stars that Clyde had brought along.

From the shadows in the hallway, Lynn watched the strange boy who seemed to know so much about stars and comets and interplanetary communication. About everything else, he seemed tongue-tied; but sitting alone with Judith, discussing Mars or Venus, he talked on and on.

They were talking so softly that Lynn could scarcely hear, and she had just started out to the kitchen when she heard Judith saying, ". . . feel sorry for Stevie. I was so cross . . ."

"I'll get him, then," the boy said, in answer. "We'll

wait till the last minute."

Lynn stood as though nailed to the floor. Judith was balking, so the warlock was going to get Stevie. It was definite. She pressed herself against the wall, all her effort straining to hear. But the conversation had changed.

"Did we really get signals from someone in outer space?" Judith was saying.

"The instruments picked up signals, but we're still not sure what caused them."

"I hope there is life out there somewhere," Judith said, and Lynn noticed the strange singsong quality that crept into her voice whenever she talked with Clyde. "I'd like to find out that there's a soul in everything, and a person could communicate with rocks and flowers and birds someday."

"Some people swear they can talk to them now," the boy told her.

"I know! I can! Honestly! Sometimes flowers lean toward me when I talk to them, as though they're really listening. And tadpoles!"

The boy smiled at Judith. "You're a witch," he said, and Judith smiled back.

Lynn went out to the kitchen, very sure of herself now. "I'll help put the dishes away," she said, and then gasped, for Mrs. Tuggle had just poured a spoonful of salt into a glass of water and was drinking it down. *They rub their bodies with parsley and belladonna, slack their thirst with salt, and are partial to the meat of babies and young children.*

The woman turned, and her face seemed strangely shriveled. The candle cast deep shadows on her chin and under her eyes, and she looked like some old crone raised up from an age long past, looking about her with beady eyes.

She caught Lynn's expression.

"Just adding a mite of salt to my water, dear. Keeps the body balanced, you know, when the weather's hot."

Lynn said nothing. She must stay calm, very calm, and watch everything that went on.

" 'Twas a strange storm we had," Mrs. Tuggle went on, wiping the last of the plates and setting them on the shelf. "A wonder it didn't take the roof off our heads."

"The porch is pretty wet," Lynn observed. "Is your grandson going to sleep out there?"

"He'll make do somewhere—on the rug, perhaps. No need to worry."

Lynn put the pots and pans away. "How long is Clyde staying with you, Mrs. Tuggle?"

"He goes back tomorrow. I'll put him on the bus myself at two o'clock."

Oh, how beautifully they had it planned. Of course! The boy would be gone by the time the Morleys came back, and Mrs. Tuggle would say he had gone back to Michigan.

"I'm going to bed now," Lynn said. "I guess I'm pretty tired, and there isn't enough light to read by."

"Will do you good, then," the old woman said, taking off her apron and hanging it over a chair. She turned to Lynn and smiled, and again the gold tooth gleamed. "Not afraid of the bogles and witches, are you? Best to take a candle to undress by, but don't set the house afire."

Lynn climbed the stairs, stopping to look in again on Stevie and then going up to the third floor, where she left her door open. Quickly she undressed, put on her pajamas, and blew out the candle.

It was almost an hour later when Judith came up. She moved so quietly that Lynn didn't even hear her footsteps. There was merely a faint glow of light from the stairs that grew brighter and brighter until at last Judith stood in the doorway with a candle in her hand. She started to go behind the curtain, stopped, looked at Lynn, and then started over.

Lynn lay still, her eyes closed, her lips slightly parted as though she were deep in sleep. For a long time, it seemed, Judith stood there, so long that Lynn's heart beat hard beneath her pajamas. She desperately wanted to look but knew she couldn't. She could sense the light from the candle through her closed eyelids. Suddenly she felt Judith's hand on her cheek. She stopped breathing. But a moment later the light moved away, and when at last she opened her eyes, Judith was on the other side of the curtain. She reached up and felt her cheek.

The scratches Judith had made that morning had now risen up in welts, and the X mark was clearly defined.

When Judith's bedspring squeaked and the candle went out, Lynn sat up quietly. She wanted to be fully alert and awake for the least little sound, the smallest flicker of light. She looked at her clock in the darkness. The illuminated hands showed 10:15. Midnight was a long way off. From the other side of the curtain came the tinkling of a bell, like chimes in a summer breeze, followed by a rush of wind in the attic above. Lynn hugged herself with her arms to stop the shaking and waited.

She leaned against the wall and tried to think of all the poetry she knew in an effort to stay awake. After that she did the multiplication tables and then the names, addresses, and birthdays of all her relatives. It was only twenty of eleven when she ran out of things to remember. She sprawled on the bed again and tried to think how it had been before the witching began—when she and Judith had made doll clothes together. They had shared lemonade stands in the summer and picnics down by Cowden's Creek. It had all been so simple and fun.

And then Judith had gone off to junior high school and by the following spring everything had changed. She had given up sewing doll clothes for sewing things for herself, and preferred Mrs. Tuggle's company to Lynn's. It was about that time that Judith had begun calling Stevie "an impossible child," and when Lynn spoke to her, she either got an answer in a faraway voice or no answer at all. And all the while Mrs. Tuggle went on sewing, sewing, in her dark little room at the top of the house, like the evil old spinning woman in *Sleeping Beauty*. . . .

"Judith!"

The voice seemed far away, and Lynn's legs and arms were numb. Her eyelids were heavy, and she realized, with horror, that she had fallen asleep after all. The whisper came again, and chills raced down her arms.

"Judith!"

Without moving, Lynn looked sleepily at the figure over by the curtain. It was the boy from Cowden's Creek, fully dressed. He had not gone to bed at all.

"What is it?" came a low voice from behind the curtain.

"It's time," whispered the boy. "I've been waiting, but you didn't come. Hurry up!"

chapter eight

The soft thud of Judith's footsteps sounded behind the curtain. To Lynn, who was barely awake, they seemed miles away, as though she herself were at the bottom of a deep well, far removed from the outside world.

She struggled to get her eyes open as she listened to the footsteps going downstairs, and tried to move her arms and legs. Pulling her head up from her pillow, she stared hard at her clock in the darkness. The illuminated hands seemed a blur in front of her eyes. She blinked and stared again. Ten minutes after midnight! She threw her legs over the side of the bed. She was late! Judith and the boy from Cowden's Creek were late. Ten past twelve, and the witches were waiting!

She groped to the top of the stairs. In the hallway below she could hear Stevie whimpering, "What is it? I'm sleepy, Judith. I don't want to go. . . ."

"Stevie!" Lynn screamed, but they had already picked him up and were carrying him down to the first floor. She had to get him before they reached the door. "Stevie! Don't go!" she screamed again, stumbling down the stairs and throwing herself at Judith. "Don't go! Help!"

Judith whirled around. "Lynn, shut up!" she snapped. "Stop that yelling!"

Lynn screamed all the harder. The boy from Cowden's Creek was moving toward the front door. "Help!" Lynn beat her fists against him and grabbed hold of Stevie's legs. "Somebody help!"

"We can't go outside with her yelling like this," the boy said to Judith, staring at Lynn.

"She's gone mad!" Judith hissed. "Absolutely mad! Lynn, be quiet or you'll have the neighbors over here."

"I want the neighbors to come! I want the police to come! You can't take Stevie! Help! Help!"

There were hurried footsteps on the stairs, and Mrs. Tuggle, in a gray robe, her hair flowing long about her wrinkled faced, rushed into the hallway. She grabbed Lynn with such force that her fingers dug deep into Lynn's shoulders.

"What on earth!" she scolded angrily. "Who awakened the girl?"

"Stevie!" screamed Lynn, finally wrestling him away from Clyde and holding him close to her. "You can't take Stevie! I'll stop all of you! I know all about what you're doing. I'll tell Mother and the neighbors and the police and—"

Mrs. Tuggle clutched Lynn's head between her hands like a steel vise and shook her.

"Stop it, girl! Stop it!"

"I won't!" cried Lynn.

"Get Stevie away from her!" Judith ordered quickly. "She's crazy. Stevie, come out here on the porch with us."

Stevie began to cry and clung harder to Lynn. "I wanna go to bed!" he wailed.

"Don't touch him!" Lynn shrieked again, and Mrs. Tuggle's hands grew even tighter on the sides of her face.

"Get the water, Judith," commanded Mrs. Tuggle. "Splash it on her forehead."

"No! No water!" Lynn hurled herself away so suddenly that she sent Mrs. Tuggle reeling against the closet door. Then, clutching Stevie in her arms, Lynn rushed into the living room and huddled beside him on the couch.

There was silence from the hallway, and then a low murmur of voices. Finally the three of them moved to the door of the living room and stood staring at Lynn. She had broken their spell. Relief flooded through her, and she felt exhausted. What would they do now? What would they say? How could they possibly explain it?

"She hit me, Mrs. Tuggle!" Judith said, sounding shocked. "She came at me hitting and scratching."

" 'Twas a bad dream you've had then, Lynn," said the old woman, searching Lynn's face closely. "Best to go to bed and sleep it off."

"It wasn't a dream!" Lynn exploded.

"What were you all about, then?" Mrs. Tuggle asked Clyde. "Up in the middle of the night?" How well she had rehearsed her lines.

"It's the Perseid meteor shower. We wanted Stevie to see it," Clyde explained. "It won't come again for a year." He went out on the front porch, Judith following. "See? It's beginning!"

"And for that you're getting a wee child up in the middle of the night?" Mrs. Tuggle scolded. "The idea!"

Lynn glared at her through narrowed eyes. "You were giving Stevie to the witches and you know it," she said deliberately.

Stevie began to whimper again.

Mrs. Tuggle sat down in a chair opposite the couch and looked at Lynn a long time before she spoke. Her eyes were small and unfriendly. "A bad dream," she said again, and shook her head. "My, my, my! Never in all my life did I see the Morley girls act so! A nightmare! That's what it was."

Lynn ignored her. She picked up Stevie and carried

him all the way up to her own bed, falling down exhausted beside him. Through the window she could see a patch of dark sky, but no stars, no meteors. Mrs. Tuggle must be furious, she thought, but Lynn was too tired to care. She sank into a fitful sleep.

The sun fell full on her face, telling her it was late in the morning. Lynn lay in exactly the same position in which she had gone to sleep the night before, and her left arm ached from being doubled up under her. She rolled over and opened her eyes. Stevie was gone, but she could hear him chattering away somewhere below.

The phone rang. Lynn got up and started downstairs. Then she remembered the boy from Cowden's Creek and put a robe on over her pajamas. Mrs. Tuggle was standing at the foot of the stairs.

"I thought I heard the phone ring," Lynn said sleepily.

" 'Twas that Beasley girl again—the third time she's called this morning, yet, and she wouldn't believe you were still asleep! She said she's coming over to see for herself! The manners of the girl!"

"What time is it?"

"Almost eleven. Clyde's been up since nine, and we've had ourselves a chore keeping Stevie quiet so you girls could sleep." She led the way to the kitchen where Stevie was drinking orange juice. Lynn could see the boy from Cowden's Creek reading the comics on the back porch. "At least the electricity is on again. I could make a proper breakfast!"

"Judith's still sleeping, then?" Lynn asked.

"That she is. After all the commotion last night, she needs it." Mrs. Tuggle put a plate of scrambled eggs on the table, but Lynn pushed it aside and reached for the cereal box instead. Mrs. Tuggle noticed and shook her head. "What a time you girls must give your dear mother. She never told me that you had nightmares."

Lynn's jaw tightened. "I had no nightmare, Mrs. Tuggle."

"Well, then, let's not talk about it," said the old woman, looking at her curiously. "But glad I was to see the light this morning. I'll be wanting bed early tonight."

Stevie remembered absolutely nothing of the night before, and when Lynn told him later that the boy from Cowden's Creek had carried him downstairs, he didn't believe it.

Lynn had just finished a bowl of Wheat Chex when Marjorie tapped on the front door and walked in.

"Boy, am I glad to see you!" she breathed, and they went immediately to the window seat in the music room. Mouse had on her Sunday clothes—a pale yellow dress and white lacy socks. Judith should see her now, Lynn was thinking. She wouldn't believe it was the same girl.

"What happened?" Mouse asked, her eyes popping

from their sockets. "Tell me *everything*—quick! I'm on my way to church."

"You'll never believe it," Lynn said dryly. "Nobody believes it. Not even Stevie."

"Tell me! Tell me!" Mouse begged.

Lynn leaned forward. "The lights went out in the storm and stayed out all night. Mrs. Tuggle managed that, I'm sure, just to make things easier for them. I put Stevie to bed and tried to stay awake, but I didn't. When I woke up, it was ten after midnight, and Clyde and Judith were trying to get Stevie out on the front porch."

Mouse gasped.

"I ran down after them and screamed and hollered, and Mrs. Tuggle said I was having a nightmare. She was really mad."

"So what did she have to say about Clyde and Judith taking Stevie outside?"

"Clyde said he wanted to show Stevie a meteor shower, but I looked out my window and didn't see a thing. It was obviously what they planned to say if anything went wrong."

"Oh, Lynn! They'll have it in for you now. What do you think they'll try next? They don't have much time if your folks will be home tonight."

"I don't know. Mrs. Tuggle said that Clyde was supposed to catch the bus for Michigan this afternoon. That was how she was going to explain his disappearance again, see. But I know they'll keep him around till they can murder Stevie some other way."

"Maybe now your mother will believe you when you tell her what happened."

"No, she won't. It will be my word against theirs. Oh, Mouse, what are we going to do?"

Mouse gave it a moment of concentrated attention. "Dig up that grave," she said.

"What?"

"Dig up the grave of Mrs. Tuggle's brother. It's the only thing left to do. We'll show that there's nobody in it, and then maybe somebody will believe us when we say that Mrs. Tuggle's brought him back bodily. Maybe we can even break her spells somehow by opening the grave."

"Mouse, do you know how long it takes to dig up a coffin?"

"A couple days, maybe?"

Lynn closed her eyes wearily. "When do we start?"

"Tomorrow. I'll call you in the morning. Right now I've got to go to church, and then we're going out to dinner. It's to celebrate my recital, see."

"How did it go?"

"Awful. I had the hiccups all the way through it, and hit the wrong key each time I hicked. But we're celebrating anyway."

As Lynn started upstairs again, Mrs. Tuggle said, "It's almost noon, Lynn, and Clyde'll be leaving soon. I thought we'd all get in my car and have us a ride to the bus station to see him off. You'd better wake Judith and tell her to come have breakfast. She'll be wanting to visit some more with him, I know, before he goes."

So the old woman was still pretending that he was leaving. Well, Lynn would play along with the game. They'd leave him there at the station, and he'd walk back to Mrs. Tuggle's where she'd keep him holed up in one of the dark rooms of her house till the time was right, and then they'd try again.

Lynn went to her own room, reluctant to face Judith and her fury. It was out in the open now. Both Judith and Mrs. Tuggle knew that Lynn knew, but they'd have to fight her tooth and nail to get Stevie.

She pulled on her clothes, took a swipe at her hair with the brush, and opened the curtain to Judith's room.

Her sister was lying on her side facing the window, her long, dark hair half covering her face.

"Judith?" Lynn said.

She stirred but did not answer.

"Judith, Mrs. Tuggle says it's time to get up. It's almost noon, and Clyde's leaving. . . ."

Slowly Judith rolled over and lay with her arms dangling down either side of the bed.

"I don't feel so good," she said, and Lynn could scarcely hear her. "I've got an awful sore throat."

Lynn stepped over to the bed. "Maybe you got cold last night," she said, and suddenly she gasped. "Judith!

You look awful! You've got measles or something!"

"Measles!" Judith's voice was more like a squeak. She sat up and reached for the mirror. There was a strange rash on her face and arms. Her eyelids were swollen, and her neck looked strangely thick.

Judith fell back on the bed and started to cry. Lynn stared, not knowing what to do. Finally she got a box of tissues from the dresser and set it on the bed.

"He's going to s—see me like this!" Judith wailed. "He's going to see me looking awful!"

"Who?"

"Clyde!" Judith sobbed. "Oh, I look terrible. And I feel miserable."

"I'd better get Mrs. Tuggle!" Lynn said. She turned and clattered downstairs. Something horrible was happening to Judith.

"Is she coming then?" Mrs. Tuggle asked.

"She's sick," said Lynn, half suspecting that the old woman knew it already.

Mrs. Tuggle stared. "Sick, is she? What's the matter with her?"

"I don't know. Measles or smallpox or something."

"Smallpox!" Mrs. Tuggle's hands rose toward the ceiling as though they were pulled by strings, and a moment later she had gathered up her apron in her arms to keep from stepping on it and was dashing up the stairs faster than Lynn had ever seen her move.

When they reached the bedroom, Judith was standing in the middle of the floor in her nightgown, staring at herself. The rash was all over her legs, too. There was a strange cast to her skin, as though it were turning yellow.

"Oh, Mrs. T—Tuggle!" she sobbed. "I'm sick!"

"Merciful heavens!" Mrs. Tuggle breathed. "Lay you down again, Judith girl. Lynn, get the thermometer."

Lynn raced to the medicine chest and back again. Judith had a temperature of 104 degrees.

"If only the Morleys were home!" Mrs. Tuggle wailed. "If I had known what would happen here, never would I have come! Listen to me, Judith. I'll be calling the doctor, but you tell me as best you can how you feel."

"I hurt all over," Judith wept, "especially my throat. My neck hurts and my stomach hurts, and I've got an awful headache."

Mrs. Tuggle hurried down to make the phone call.

"Lynn," said Judith weakly. "Tell Clyde good-bye for me. Tell him I'm sorry I can't see him before he leaves."

"Okay," Lynn said awkwardly. Was she dying then?

". . . and . . . and give him this," Judith said. She reached under her pillow and pulled out the yellow ribbon that Lynn had seen in the cemetery.

"Why?" Lynn asked, curious.

"It's important, that's all."

Lynn went downstairs carrying the ribbon. Clyde was standing in the hallway, listening to Mrs. Tuggle talking on the phone.

"What's the matter with Judith?" he asked Lynn.

"I don't know. She's awfully sick. She asked me to give this to you and says she's sorry she can't see you before you leave."

The boy's face flushed. He stuffed the ribbon in his back pocket without a word.

Mrs. Tuggle put down the phone. "Fancy that! The doctor won't be home till this evening! Out of town, he is, and if it's urgent I'm to take the girl to the hospital. Now wouldn't Mrs. Morley like to come home and find her daughter in a hospital?"

Stevie heard the commotion and came in from the kitchen. "What's the matter?"

"Judith's sick," Lynn answered.

"And best you don't go up there bothering her," Mrs. Tuggle told him. She turned to Clyde. "Go back to the house, lad. You'll have to pack up yourself and not be leaving anything behind. I'll call a neighbor friend and have him drive you to the bus."

She came forward and kissed the boy on the cheek, giving his arm a pinch. "Do you well now in school, and write to your granny when there's a moment wanting."

"I will," Clyde said uncomfortably. "Thanks for letting me come."

"Good-bye, then. You wait for Mr. Simpkins. I'll ask him to come by at 1:30."

She picked up the phone again to make her call, and the boy from Cowden's Creek, with his strange blue eyes and maps and books of the stars and heavens, walked out the front door and down the steps. Lynn could see a piece of Judith's yellow ribbon hanging from his pants pocket.

It was almost seven that evening when Mr. and Mrs. Morley returned. Mother took one step in the door, looked at the faces around her, and said instantly, "What happened?"

See? Lynn told herself. *If it weren't for Judith getting sick, I might have run right over to Mother and told her everything about last night. Mrs. Tuggle knew I would. Now everybody's worried about Judith. They won't pay any attention to me. Mrs. Tuggle thinks I'll forget about it, but I won't.*

"It's Judith, Mrs. Morley," Mrs. Tuggle said before Lynn could open her mouth. Lynn marveled at the concerned tone of her voice. What an actress!

"Where is she? What's wrong?" Mother said, dropping her overnight bag on the floor.

"She's upstairs and very sick. The doctor's been gone all day, but he's on his way over now. We'll know something soon, don't you worry."

Mrs. Morley's shoes went flying into the living room and a moment later she was running upstairs in her stocking feet. Father came in carrying another bag. He took one look at Mrs. Tuggle and said, "What happened?"

The second overnight bag dropped to the floor, and Mr. Morley went upstairs. And then the doctor arrived. Lynn sat on the sofa and held Stevie on her lap. What if Judith died? What if the witches were so angry at losing Stevie that they took Judith instead? What if Mrs. Tuggle were giving Judith away just to appease them?

Twenty minutes later, the doctor and Mr. Morley came back down together and shook hands at the front door.

"What's wrong with her, Dad?" Lynn asked as soon as the doctor was gone.

"He thinks it's mononucleosis. He took some blood samples, and we'll know for sure tomorrow. Thank goodness, it doesn't seem to be anything worse, but she's a really sick girl, I'll tell you."

"It sounds terrible," Lynn ventured.

Mr. Morley came over, picked up Stevie, and slung him over his shoulder playfully, giving him a swat on the bottom. "She'll feel pretty low for a few weeks, I imagine, but she should be able to start school in September if she takes it easy. She'll need a lot of rest and quiet. You got that, son? Quiet. That means you."

Mother came back downstairs with Mrs. Tuggle and collapsed in a chair by the sofa. Stevie jumped on her lap, and she cuddled him while she talked. "Well, I suppose it could be worse," she said. "It's strange, but last night I had the feeling that something was going wrong back home. I resisted the impulse to call, because I knew you had my number and would call me at the conference if you needed me. It was some time in the night. I can't remember just when. But . . . better to come home to mononucleosis than find the house burned down or the children gone or something."

Lynn looked at Mrs. Tuggle. The old woman did not return her glance but kept her eyes straight ahead.

"Tell me, then," Mrs. Tuggle said, changing the subject, "did you have a good meeting?"

"It was simply marvelous!" Mother said. "A whole weekend with writers and editors and librarians! They want me to come back again next year for a whole week and teach a full course. I'd love to do it."

"She did a good job with her lecture, too," Mr. Morley put in. "Can take me along any time she wants. That's a fringe benefit of being married to a writer, I guess."

"So how did you all manage, other than Judith's getting sick?" Mother asked. She looked over at Lynn. "Anything exciting happen?"

Now was her chance. Now—with Mrs. Tuggle here—face-to-face . . .

"Mo—ther!" came Judith's voice faintly from upstairs. "Could I have some aspirin for this headache?"

Mrs. Morley jumped up. "Poor dear. We'll make a bed for her down in the dining room where we can wait on her. Lynn, it looks as if you're going to be our nurse for the next couple weeks, doesn't it?"

There was no time on Monday to dig up the grave. Mother was finishing the last chapter of her book and wanted to get it all down on paper while the ideas were fresh. Later she would go over it again and again, re-writing it three or four times before she considered it actually done. She put Lynn in charge of everything, but spent an extra long lunch hour each day fixing special soups for Judith and rubbing her back or reading her funny letters and news clippings that she thought would amuse her.

Strange, Lynn was thinking one afternoon, but Judith hadn't said one word about the awful night Mother was gone. She had expected a fierce quarrel, but Judith seemed to have no strength to discuss it or anything else that took a lot of words. Was it possible that Judith didn't even remember it? Was this Mrs. Tuggle's doing?

"About that grave . . ." Mouse said impatiently Wednesday when she called.

"I can't this week," Lynn told her. "I've got to take care of Judith. I promised I'd read to her this afternoon because her eyes hurt. Wait till she's better. . . ."

It was a different Judith who lay on the daybed in the dining room, tremblingly eating a bowl of soup, or shuffling slowly to the bathroom and back, scarcely speaking above a whisper.

"Thank you," she murmured when Lynn picked up something she had dropped or brought her a cool orange drink made in the blender. Mrs. Morley bought a macramé kit and instruction book, and when Judith began to feel stronger, she and Lynn sat on the daybed knotting belts and purses from the biege-colored string.

All the while they sat together chatting, Lynn studied her sister. Before the events of the summer, Lynn would have described Judith as selfish, arrogant, rude, and cold. She would have said that Judith was that way because she wanted to be. Now she was not so sure. Whether or not Judith had been possessed, she had always been a different person from Lynn, and would go on all her life being different. There were dozens of reasons why people did what they did—why some were followers and some were not, for example.

The fact was, however, that people could change, too. Judith was changing. Lynn herself was beginning to feel different, but she was not sure just how, or what it meant.

"You know, Mouse," Lynn said one day, "I think I know what's happened. Judith lost her power when she got sick. Mrs. Tuggle saw that her plan wouldn't work, so she just gave up on Judith. She made her sick so it would take our attention. She hoped we'd forget what happened, and I honestly think Judith has. But I won't. Not ever."

"You could be right," Mouse said. "Maybe Judith lost her only chance, and Mrs. Tuggle will have to find somebody else. But I still think we ought to dig up that grave."

Four days before school began, Judith was feeling very much better. She still took a rest in the middle of the afternoon, but her temperature was down and she was walking around and even going out some again. She brought her newly made school clothes down from Mrs. Tuggle's, all ready for the new semester. When Lynn went upstairs to take her a letter, she was sweeping her room with the broom and straightening out her dresser. She didn't even grumble at Lynn for coming in without asking.

"It says C. T. on the corner," Lynn said, dropping the envelope on the bed. "I suppose that's Clyde Tuggle."

"I suppose," said Judith, and went on with her sweeping. She was going out that afternoon with a new boy she'd met at the library, and there was no time for letter reading now. Lynn noticed that the ring she had been wearing on her finger for several weeks was gone.

Stevie had been invited to go to the park with some neighbors, so Lynn and Marjorie had the afternoon to themselves. It was somewhat cooler than usual. The air had a crispness about it that spoke of fall and school and change. And soon vacation would be over. It was a day for just remembering and feeling and being, and doing nothing in particular. The girls sat on the front porch, looking out over the September haze that seemed to envelop the street.

"What do you think she's doing now?" Mouse said.

"Who?"

"Mrs. Tuggle."

"Probably sitting up in her window with a spyglass, looking around for a new girl," said Lynn.

They were silent for a moment.

"Boy, I'll bet she's really got it in for you," Mouse said finally. "If it weren't for you, think of the power she'd have. You'll never want to visit her again, will you?"

Lynn shifted uneasily. "It's strange, but I feel I will somehow."

"Lynn!"

"I know. It doesn't make sense. Maybe it's curiosity. I'm not sure. But I have this weird feeling that I've got to find out the whys of Mrs. Tuggle. In fact, I'd like to go up there right now and see if she hasn't got Clyde hidden away in one of those rooms."

"Lynn! You don't know what you're saying!"

"Don't you feel a sort of pull when you think of Mrs. Tuggle's house?"

"No! I feel a push. Backward. I wouldn't go there again for a million dollars!"

Lynn stood up. "How about fifty cents? I'll give you a Kennedy half dollar if you'll go up to her house with me and ask to use the bathroom."

"How many times can we ask to use her bathroom without making her suspicious?" Mouse croaked.

"Well, we'll say that Judith thinks she left some of her clothes, then, and ask to go up to the sewing room and check."

"She'll follow us upstairs!"

"At least we can look around and listen for footsteps. If Clyde's there, we might find a clue."

"Okay. Fifty cents," sighed Mouse, and they went down to the street below and started up the steep hill.

Lynn was quiet as they walked along. She had never told her mother what had happened that night. She was tired of telling and not being believed. If Mrs. Tuggle's claim on Judith was released by her illness, Lynn would never bring up the subject again. But if Judith began going back to Mrs. Tuggle's, or other things began happening that no one could explain, Lynn would tell her everything.

"Think the witches will come and carry *her* off?" Mouse said at last, breaking the silence.

"Who?"

"Mrs. Tuggle. Maybe they're so mad at losing Stevie and then Judith that they'll take her instead."

"It wouldn't work. She doesn't have enough fat for anything."

"That's something I always wondered about, Lynn. What do you suppose they do with it, anyway—all that fat? It doesn't take that much to grease a broomstick."

"Make candles out of it, I suppose, to dance around at midnight. Maybe we should just ask her right out: 'Mrs. Tuggle, what do you witches do with all that fat?'"

At first they thought she wasn't home. Lynn knocked,

and then after a minute, Mouse rapped loudly with the ghoulish-looking knocker. They were turning away to peep in the window when the door opened slowly, creaking as though it were blown open by the wind, and in the darkness of the inner hallway they could see the old woman's eyes glistening from her small wrinkled face.

"Come in," she said, and smiled as soon as she saw Lynn. "I was expecting you."

"You were?" asked Lynn in a whisper.

Mrs. Tuggle led the way to the kitchen. "I've been canning peaches all week, and your mother said she'd send you up sometime to get a few jars. Make a good cobbler, they will, come winter."

The girls still needed an excuse to go upstairs and look around.

"Judith wasn't sure she got all her clothes from your sewing room," Lynn said. "I told her we'd come up and check."

The old woman turned around and looked at the girls intently. Then she smiled knowingly, and her gold tooth glinted in the light.

"Of course, do go look."

Lynn and Mouse moved quietly up the stairs. From below, Mrs. Tuggle began her strange crooning. "This may be our last chance to look around," Lynn whispered. "If you see anything at all suspicious, remember it."

They were almost at the top of the stairs when they heard the footsteps. They were not overhead this time, but on the very floor where the girls were standing. The bathroom door was closed and there was the sound of running water in the basin.

Lynn and Marjorie flattened themselves against the wall in the upper hallway, fingers digging in each other's arms.

"What will we say when he comes out?" Mouse whispered. "Boo?"

"I—I don't know. What if it's not Clyde? What if it's somebody else she's conjured up? Mrs. Elfreda Lewis or somebody?"

The water stopped. There were footsteps again. The bathroom door opened and a shadow fell on the wall outside—a tall shadow, taller than Clyde.

And suddenly Mrs. Morley stepped out into the hall.

"Lynn! What in the world are you girls doing up here?"

"W—we came to see if Judith left any clothes," Lynn stammered.

"Well, I'm glad you're here, because dear Mrs. Tuggle has been canning peaches and wants to give us some. You can help me carry them home." Lynn's mother looked radiant. "Guess what! I finished the first draft of my book, and I'm giving myself the afternoon off." She put one arm around each girl and walked back downstairs with them. "Oh, I feel glorious! I finished the book, and I'm free! Free! Free!"

Mother always said she was free when she finished a book, even though she'd spend the next two months rewriting it.

"It's not perfect yet by any means," she continued excitedly, "but I just know it's going to be a good one. Really!"

They picked up the peaches in the kitchen, two jars apiece, and Mrs. Morley thanked Mrs. Tuggle again. They went back out through the big front door, which closed slowly behind them, but not all the way—and the old woman watched them through the crack with small beady eyes.

"It's a different kind of book this time," Mrs. Morley began as they started down the brick sidewalk, Lynn on one side of her, Mouse on the other. "You see, it starts out with . . ."

Mouse liked a good story and was a willing listener, but Lynn knew better. Mrs. Morley would talk on and on.

"We were just on our way somewhere, Mother," she said. "I mean, we've got things to do. Maybe you could tell us about the book some other time."

"What were you going to do?" asked Mother.

"Well—uh—ummmm—dig up a grave, maybe," Lynn said desperately.

"Ah! You see? You're responsible for my story, you two! That's why I want you to be the first to hear it.

You see, in the beginning, Ann Bridges suspects that her sister Elsie is a witch, and all kinds of things happen. I can't begin to tell you everything. . . ."

Lynn and Marjorie turned slowly toward each other, their eyes wide, but Mrs. Morley moved on down the brick sidewalk, bobbing and swaying.

"And there's an old woman in the book—of course it's really Mrs. Tuggle—whom Ann believes is responsible for putting a hex on her sister. Somehow Ann gets the idea that the old woman is going to set fire to the house. There's just so much, and the plot is all woven up in witchcraft and superstition. Don't you think it will be marvelous?"

"I—I don't know," Mouse stammered.

"But then—at the very end—guess what happens?" Mother rattled on as though the girls weren't even there. They had reached the Morley house and had gone on into the kitchen to put the peaches on the table. Mother lowered her voice to a whisper: "At the very end, in a horribly scary scene with the old woman and Ann alone together, their two shadows mingling in the light of the candle, Ann discovers that it is not really Elsie after all who is becoming a witch, but she herself; and when she looks in the mirror, she sees, instead, the face of the old woman."

Like the two lidless angels in the cemetery, Lynn and Mouse stood like chunks of marble, neither moving nor speaking—their eyes unblinking, their lips wide open.

The horror settled slowly down upon them, like the September haze rolling in from Cowden's Creek.

But Mrs. Morley didn't even notice. "I'm going to bake a pie and celebrate!" she said, stepping out of her sandals and padding barefoot about the kitchen. "Thanks for helping me with the peaches, girls. It's a glorious afternoon, isn't it?"

Slowly Lynn and Marjorie moved out of the kitchen, through the door, and down the sidewalk to the steep steps, where they sat together side by side, linked in a common trance. A shadow fell over the street, over the old brick sidewalks, and the gabled houses. Somewhere from the sky over Cowden's Creek, a crow cawed, then another, and the girls turned their faces toward the house on the hill where an old woman waited.

Masterful mysteries
by
PHYLLIS REYNOLDS NAYLOR

(Winner of the Edgar Allan Poe Award)

☐ **NIGHT CRY**   40017-1 $3.25
Scaredy-cat Ellen Stump <u>really</u> has something
to worry about when a suspicious stranger
starts hanging around her house just after a
local boy is kidnapped

☐ **THE WITCH HERSELF**   40044-9 $2.95
Lynn and her best friend Mouse are terrified
when Lynn's mother sets up an office in the
home of a dangerous witch!

☐ **THE WITCH'S SISTER**   40028-7 $2.95
Lynn is convinced her sister, Judith, is a witch—
especially after she sees her conjure up a real
live boy from the middle of a lake!

☐ **WITCH WATER**   40038-4 $2.95
Lynn and Mouse are off on another
witch hunt—only this time it's a spooky
old neighbor that they're after...